THE MAGIC
OF CHRISTMAS

BY
SARAH MORGAN

™MILLS & BOON®

Pure reading pleasure

All the characters in this book have no existence outside the imagination of the author, and have no relation whatsoever to anyone bearing the same name or names. They are not even distantly inspired by any individual known or unknown to the author, and all the incidents are pure invention.

First published in Great Britain 2007
Harlequin Mills & Boon Limited,
Eton House, 18-24 Paradise Road, Richmond, Surrey TW9 1SR

© Sarah Morgan 2007

ISBN: 978 0 263 85272 1

Set in Times Roman 10½ on 12¼ pt
03-1107-49248

Printed and bound in Spain
by Litografia Rosés, S.A., Barcelona

THE MAGIC
OF CHRISTMAS

CHAPTER ONE

'YOU'RE going to fall in love with a strong, handsome man, dear. And he's going to propose to you on Christmas Day.'

'I hate to disappoint you, but all the men I meet are either sick or injured and there's no way I'm marrying any of them.' Lara applied the last of the Steristrips to the woman's leg and glanced at her patient with laughter in her eyes. 'Anyway, the last thing I need right now is love.'

'Everyone needs love.'

'You sound exactly like my mother,' Lara murmured, checking the wound one last time. 'And I'm not disagreeing, I'm just saying that this is a bad time. I've resigned from my job and I'm going travelling in January. I'm visiting my brother. He's been gone for six months and I miss him horribly.'

'Yes, Australia is a long way.'

'How do you know that he's living in Australia?' Startled, Lara looked up from the wound and her patient gave a placid smile.

'I'm a psychic, dear. Seeing the future is what I do. I was on my way to do a Christmas party when I slipped. The pavements are very icy today.' She drew her beaded scarf around her shoulders and studied Lara closely. 'Your aura is red—the colour of strength and passion.'

'Well, I have no objection to passion or to meeting a strong handsome man.' Trying to work out how the woman could possibly know that her brother was living in Australia, Lara reached for a dressing. 'I could do with a bit of excitement in my life. But no man, however gorgeous, is going to stop me going to Australia.'

'Not stop, no. But you'll be cutting your trip short. You won't want to be without him.'

'Thea, you have to stop this!' Lara stared at her patient with a mixture of amusement and exasperation. 'From the moment the paramedics brought you in, you've been predicting everyone's future. You've already shocked Fran on Reception by telling her that she's going to be pregnant by Christmas.'

'Why is that shocking?'

'Because she doesn't even have a boyfriend! You have to admit that single to pregnant in less than a month is a bit of a leap even for the broad-minded.' She carefully placed the dressing over the wound and secured it with a light compression bandage. 'There. That's done. You can go home.'

And so could she. It was her half-day and there was somewhere she needed to be.

'I'm not going anywhere until I've read your palm. I want to repay your kindness to me. It's the least I can do. I might be able to give you some clarity.' The woman reached out and took Lara's hand in a firm grip. 'Let me see…'

Amused, Lara gave her hand a little tug. 'My hand is going to tell you that I'm a single, overworked nurse who doesn't have time for romance.'

'Love often arrives when you're not looking for it,' Thea murmured, holding Lara's palm in a firm grip. 'Oh, my dear girl, you're so lonely, aren't you? You work so hard that you don't have a social life, you're tired all the time and deep down you dream of having a big, noisy family of your own. You can't understand why everyone seems to be in a couple, apart from you. You're asking yourself if you're too fussy.'

Lara sat for a moment, trying not to be spooked by the accuracy of the woman's assessment. She gave herself a mental shake. 'I have bags under my eyes so it's obvious that I'm tired. I'm a nurse in the busiest emergency department in London, so it's obvious that I'm going to be working too hard to have a social life. It's not rocket science. I don't know how you found out about the ticket to Australia, but plenty of people go there so it was just a lucky guess.'

It had to have been a lucky guess.

Ignoring Lara's brisk interjection, Thea continued to scrutinise her palm. 'You're dreading Christmas because this is the first year that the whole of your family won't be together and you're feeling sad about that.'

Lara felt her heart twist and she stood up suddenly and snatched her hand away. 'Go back to your GP in five days to have the dressing taken off.'

Thea gave a gentle smile. 'You're wondering how I know so much about you, aren't you? You're telling yourself that I'm just a silly old lady talking mumbo-jumbo.'

'Thea—'

'What can I possibly know? But, you see, I *do* know. I can read the future. Wonderful things are going to happen to you this Christmas. A wonderful man. Four children.'

'*Four* children?' Lara shook her head and started to laugh. 'Well, that's going to be relaxing.'

'You have plenty to laugh about.' Thea stood up and adjusted her coat. 'Your future is with a strong, handsome man who is sexier than sin. Plenty of women have wanted him but you're the one he's going to spend his life with. Women are going to envy you.'

Lara washed her hands, wondering why she found the woman's words so disturbing when it was all nonsense. 'And where am I going to meet this gorgeous specimen of manhood?' Keeping her tone light, she tugged paper towels out of the dispenser with more force than was necessary. 'Will he be lying under my Christmas tree?'

'Sometimes you have to look for love and sometimes it just finds you.' Thea glanced around her with interest. 'He's already here, waiting for you around the corner.'

The door to the treatment room flew open and one of the emergency department sisters stuck her head into the room. 'Lara? I need you in Resus right now. Are you nearly finished here or shall I find someone to take over?'

Resus? *So much for her half-day.*

Lara dropped the towel in the bin. 'I've finished, Jane.' She turned to Thea. 'Do you need to call someone to give you a lift home?'

Thea reached calmly for her bag. 'I booked a taxi when I woke up this morning. I knew I was going to fall so I thought I might as well arrange my transport home from hospital.'

Thoroughly unsettled, Lara just about managed a smile. 'Right. Well…' She cleared her throat. 'You need to come back in five days to have that wound checked, or go to your GP. Don't forget to keep that leg up.'

'And don't you forget what I said.' Thea walked slowly towards the door, limping slightly. 'Mr Right is waiting for you around the corner, in this very department. He's the path to your happiness. I've seen it all in your palm.'

'I'll remember,' Lara waited for Thea to leave the room and then followed Jane into the corridor.

'What on earth was that about?' Jane tucked her pen back into her pocket as they hurried towards Resus. 'What's supposed to be in your palm? Tell me it's not MRSA. There shouldn't be anything in your palm if you're washing your hands properly.'

'Apparently my palm holds the answers to my future. My patient was a psychic. She told Jack, the paramedic, that his wife is going to have a boy, even though the ultrasound has already confirmed it's a girl. She told Fran that she's going to be pregnant by Christmas, and apparently Mr Right, who just happens to be strong and handsome, is waiting for me around the corner.' Lara glanced at her watch. 'Unfortunately for my empty stomach, my future didn't seem to include lunch and at the moment I'd swap a lifetime with Mr Right-around-the-corner for a decent meal.'

'You're going to meet Mr Right?' Jane's face brightened and Lara threw her an incredulous look.

'Oh, yes, of course I am. After all, the emergency department is such a perfect setting for romance, don't you think? I've always had a thing for violent drunks.'

Jane shrugged. 'You can joke, but what is life without hope?'

'I think it's called reality. Oh, and apparently I'm going to have four children.'

'*Four?*'

'I know.' Lara smiled and shook her head. 'It's enough to make a girl faint, isn't it? The thought alone is enough to have me booking a spa day.'

Another ED sister hurried up to Jane, in search of the keys to the drug cupboard, and Jane unpinned them from her uniform, still talking to Lara. 'Why are you so sceptical? Given that you're off to Australia, this would be a very bad time for you to meet a man.' She handed the keys to her colleague. 'So it's inevitable that you're going to meet one. That's the way life works.'

'You're a jaded cynic. And it doesn't matter if I do meet a man because it usually takes me less than one date to spot all the reasons why we'd be totally miserable together.'

They walked quickly down the corridor together, weaving through patients who were making their way around the hospital.

'You're far too picky.' Jane glanced at her. 'What was wrong with that registrar from Paeds? I liked him.'

'Too earnest. After a hard day working in the ED, I don't want an exhausting date.'

'So how about the physio with glasses? He adored you and he was *really* fit.'

'He wanted me to meet his mother.'

'That's a good thing!'

'Not after one date.' Lara suppressed a yawn. 'And he had a really wet mouth. I can't have a long-term relationship with someone with a wet mouth.'

'Lara.' Jane's tone was exasperated. 'You'll never meet anyone if you don't lower your standards.'

'But that's just it,' Lara said softly, pausing for a moment. 'When I eventually get married, I want it to be because I'm really in love, not because I'm desperate. My parents have just celebrated their thirtieth wedding anniversary and they're still crazy about each other. That's what I want. And I'm not going to get that if I settle for someone who irritates me.'

'But you don't give a man a chance! If you only date someone once or twice, how can you be sure that they're not "the one"?'

'Because if they're driving me crackers after twenty

minutes then it's a fair assumption that we're not going to make twenty years,' Lara said dryly. 'The truth is I'd rather be happily single than unhappily married. Anyway, enough of my loveless life. What's happening in Resus?'

'Young woman with chest pains and shortness of breath. And, if Mr Right is waiting round the corner, I don't think it's a match made in heaven because he certainly isn't strong or handsome. Last time I looked he was twenty-two stone, covered in tattoos and completely stoned. I've already called Security.'

'You see what I mean? I always attract the good ones. It's the reason I'm single.' Lara pushed open the doors of Resus and stopped dead, her breath catching in her throat as her eyes settled on the doctor on the other side of the room.

Christian Blake.

He was standing by the trolley, his head angled slightly as he listened to the patient talk. His hair was glossy dark, his eyes a deep blue and his body strong and powerful. He wore the same regulation scrub suit that everyone wore in the ED, but on him the usually unflattering garment looked as though it had been designed specifically to display his superior masculine attributes.

Lara allowed herself the luxury of a brief glance at his athletic physique and then she looked away.

He was the senior consultant. *A colleague.*

And he was also—

'Why does he have to be married?' Jane muttered in an undertone, and Lara gave an exaggerated sigh of regret.

'Because the world is a cruel, hard place,' she muttered back. 'And, anyway, it doesn't make any difference in my case, because men like him always trample over me as they rush to embrace the tall, blonde stick with the perfect hair who just happens to be standing behind me. And, if by some strange chance he did happen to notice me, it would take me less than a minute to start finding his faults because that's what I do.' With a fatalistic shrug she let the door swing shut behind her and walked into the room.

A strong, handsome man who is sexier than sin.

For some reason, the psychic's words played on her mind and Lara's heart performed a series of strange rhythms. Well, they certainly didn't come any sexier than Christian. Ever since he'd taken up his post as senior consultant in the ED two months earlier, all the women in the hospital had been hoping and dreaming.

Except her.

She was about to embark on the trip of a lifetime.

Even if Christian hadn't been married, she wouldn't have been interested. But that didn't stop her admiring him.

'If you're looking for perfection, I think you've just found it,' Jane murmured, and Lara frowned at her as she slid past her into the room.

'He's married. If I want pain, I'll just go ahead and remove my heart with a blunt scalpel and have done with it.' She walked briskly across the resuscitation room. 'Good afternoon, Dr Blake.'

He looked up, his gaze cool and assessing. 'Lara, this is Ellen Bates.' He spoke with characteristic brevity, delivering the necessary facts and nothing more. 'She's thirty-two years of age and complaining of chest pain and shortness of breath.'

He never showed the slightest flicker of emotion, Lara mused as she smiled at the patient and reached for a blood-pressure cuff. He gave nothing away. He'd been working in the emergency department for two months and during that time he'd shown no inclination to socialise with the staff or reveal intimate facts about himself. On one occasion his daughter had phoned the department, and that had been how they'd discovered that he was married with children. Apart from that one incident, nothing. He worked. He went home—no doubt, to his beautiful wife. *Because Lara had absolutely no doubt that a man this impossibly handsome would have an equally impossibly beautiful wife.*

The patient's eyes were fixed on Christian's face. 'I was at the office Christmas lunch and then all of a sudden I started to feel terrible. Typical. The first time for ages I actually get to eat lunch and I'm ill. Usually I'm too busy working to bother.'

'Has anything like this ever happened before?'

'I do get palpitations occasionally,' Ellen murmured, her face screwed up as she rubbed the flat of her hand against her chest. 'But I've always assumed they're caused by the amount of coffee and diet cola I consume. I'm a lawyer. I spend whole days in boring meetings and caffeine is the only thing that keeps me conscious.'

Lara quickly attached her to the machine and checked her observations. Seeing that Ellen's pulse was two hundred, she glanced at Christian and he nodded to indicate that he'd seen the reading.

'I want to get a line in and take some bloods.'

Knowing that they needed to check the patient's blood oxygen level, Lara swiftly attached the necessary probe to Ellen's finger and then picked up the IV tray. 'Is there anyone you'd like me to call, Ellen?'

'No one.' Ellen didn't look in her direction. Her eyes were occupied with studying the dark stubble that shaded Christian's hard, angular jaw.

'Can we check her sats, please, Lara?' Christian slid the venflon into the vein and released the tourniquet.

'Just doing it now.' Lara adjusted the probe and watched the machine. 'Sats are ninety-eight per cent.'

'Good. These can go to the lab.' He dropped the blood bottles onto the tray. 'I'll do the forms in a minute.'

Lara handed him some tape so that he could secure the venflon, her eyes still watching the pulse and blood-pressure readings. 'She's still tachycardic.'

Christian's gaze followed hers and he moved the IV tray, reached for his stethoscope and hooked it into his ears.

'I'm just going to listen to your chest, Ellen.'

Ellen lowered her eyelashes in an unmistakably flirtatious gesture. 'Anytime. I suppose the one good thing about all this is having you leaning over me. I thought doctors as good-looking and sexy as you only appeared on television. Are you real or have they flown you in from Hollywood to perk up everyone's Christmas?'

In the process of labelling blood bottles, Lara winced slightly at the patient's less than subtle approach and glanced towards Christian, anticipating a cool putdown.

But he chose not to respond to the comment. *He was probably used to female adulation,* Lara thought to herself as she dropped the bottles into the bag and handed them to another nurse to take to the lab. He was so impossibly attractive he had to have been fending off desperately hopeful women all of his adult life.

She pulled the ECG machine closer to the trolley and tried to ignore the fact that Ellen was still flirting with Christian.

'Do you play poker?' Her voice was husky. 'I bet you do. You have one of those faces that gives nothing away. Inscrutable. You must win millions. Oh, dear.' She closed her eyes. 'I feel horribly, horribly dizzy. And sadly I don't think it's anything to do with the fact that a gorgeous man is listening to my chest.'

Wondering whether she'd even noticed anyone other

than Christian, Lara ripped open some pads. 'I just need to attach these to your chest, Ellen, so that we can get a reading of your heart rate.'

Ellen didn't look at her.

'Pulse is two hundred and twenty,' Lara said, her eyes flickering to the monitor as she swiftly and competently attached the electrodes to the patient. 'Do you want me to call the cardiologists?'

Christian looped the stethoscope back around his neck and gave a swift nod. 'Please.'

Ellen clutched his arm, her outward appearance of calm slipping. 'Am I having a heart attack?'

'We need to perform some tests before we make a diagnosis, but I don't think you're having a heart attack, Ellen.' His gaze flickered to Lara just as she switched on the machine. 'Are you ready to do a trace?'

'Coming right up.'

Ellen gave a whimper and shifted on the trolley. 'I feel all sweaty and clammy. Oh, God, something awful is happening, isn't it? I knew I'd been working too hard lately.'

'Try not to panic,' Lara murmured, but Ellen didn't even look in her direction. It was clear that all her hope for the future was fixed on Christian, who was studying the ECG machine. It purred softly as it produced a trace and he watched for a moment, his eyes narrowed. 'Her ECG is showing regular narrow complex tachycardia with retrograde P waves.'

Interested, Lara leaned forward to take a closer look. 'Mmm. There's a shortened PR interval and a delta wave.'

Christian glanced at her in astonishment. 'Yes,' he murmured, 'there is.'

'So…' *Why was he staring at her?* 'Do you want to try adenosine or go straight for cardioversion?' She knew that some doctors were reluctant to give adenosine in the emergency setting.

He was still staring. 'We'll give her 6 milligrams of adenosine by rapid IV push and see if we can get her back into sinus rhythm.' He paused and she nodded to indicate that she understood that there was always the chance that the patient might develop a life-threatening arrhythmia.

'So we'll just have this within grabbing distance,' she said quietly, moving the defibrillator next to the trolley.

Then she prepared the drug and handed it to Christian, who checked it and inserted the syringe into the venflon.

'What's happening?' Ellen moaned, rubbing her hand over her chest. 'What's happening?'

'Ellen, the conduction system of your heart isn't working properly and your heart is being overstimulated. That's why you're feeling the way you are. The drug I'm giving you should prevent some of the electrical impulses getting through and slow the heart.' Christian depressed the syringe to push the drug into the vein then dropped the empty syringe onto the tray next to him.

'I'll do you a rhythm strip,' Lara said, programming the ECG machine and then standing to one side so that he could see the printout.

Ellen gave a sigh. 'I'm feeling a bit better. But my face feels really hot.'

'That's a side effect of the drug we just gave you. Nothing to worry about.' Christian's gaze flickered to the monitor. 'I'm going to refer you to the cardiologists, Ellen. They'll want to do some more tests.'

'Do you know what's wrong?'

He looped the stethoscope back around his neck. 'The electric currents that control your heart aren't working properly. Put simply, they're taking a short cut.'

'I'm a lawyer. I don't need the simple version.'

Christian studied her for a moment. 'All right. Do you know anything about normal conduction pathways in the heart?'

'No, but I'm a fast learner.'

Christian pulled a piece of paper and a pen out of his pocket and swiftly drew a diagram. 'In the normal heart, electrical impulses start in the sino-atrial node in the right atrium—the atria are the chambers at the top of your heart—' his pen flew over the page to illustrate his point '—and pass through the atrioventricular node to the ventricles in the bottom of your heart. The atrioventricular node limits the electrical activity that passes through to the ventricles and acts as a break on the heart rate. That's what happens in the normal heart.'

Ellen looked at the drawing and gave a hollow laugh. 'And that's not me, right?'

'Sometimes there's an extra electrical pathway that bypasses the normal process and conducts electricity at a higher rate—there's no filter, if you like. The result is that the heart can beat very quickly and that causes the symptoms you felt today.'

Lara studied the ECG again. 'If she has an accessory pathway, why does the QRS complex look normal?'

'Because ventricular depolarisation can occur through the normal pathway. It's a combination of pre-excitation and normal conduction.'

'You've lost me.' Ellen sighed. 'So how did I get this extra pathway? Was I born with it?'

'Yes, it's congenital. Some people have more than one. Basically it happens when the atria and the ventricles fail to separate completely.'

'But why hasn't it been picked up before?'

'Because the majority of the time the normal pathway is used.'

'And can it be fixed?'

'Extremely successfully.' Christian folded the ECG strip and attached it to the notes. 'We'll refer you to the cardiologists and they'll carry out electrophysiological studies—basically, looking at the conduction of your heart.'

Ellen frowned. 'And then?'

'If they think you're an appropriate candidate, then they may do something called radiofrequency ablation—to put it simply, they destroy the extra electrical pathway by sending an electric current through it.'

'Sounds scary.'

'Actually, it's a very successful procedure. It takes a few hours and requires an overnight stay in hospital, but no more than that.'

Ellen gave a wan smile. 'I'm not allowed time off in my job. Even sleeping is banned.'

'Sounds familiar,' Lara murmured, watching as Christian scribbled on the notes. Over the past two months, she'd developed enormous respect for him. No matter what the situation, he never lost his cool. He was focused and skilled and didn't let emotion cloud his judgement.

Lara studied him for a moment, wondering whether he was even aware of Ellen's advances.

As if to test the theory, the woman gave him a smile that was pure invitation. 'If I'm in hospital, will you visit me? I never get to meet anyone except boring lawyers in my job. I bet you only ever meet boring nurses.'

'That's me,' Lara said lightly, slipping the tourniquet back into her pocket. 'Boring nurse.'

Ellen turned her head and looked at her, as if only now noticing that there was someone else in the room with

Christian. Her eyes widened as she stared at Lara. 'Boring maybe, but beautiful,' she muttered with a faint smile. 'How do you manage to look so good in that shapeless blue thing? I dress in designer wear from head to foot and I don't manage to look as good as you. Who does your hair? It's fabulous.'

'My hair?' Taken aback by the question, it took Lara a moment to answer. 'No one. Most of the time *I* don't even do it. I mean, I wake up with it looking like this. That's when my job allows me the luxury of sleep, which isn't often.'

Ellen gave a wry smile. 'Your job sounds a lot like mine. Except that I don't look a fraction as beautiful as you even after eleven undisturbed hours of sleep. Someone must do your colour. Those blonde streaks are gorgeous. So natural.'

'That's because they *are* natural,' Lara muttered, wondering why she was discussing her hair with a patient. In the circumstances it seemed utterly bizarre. Any moment now they'd be talking about shoes. Bracing herself for a sharp comment from Christian about her lack of professionalism, her eyes slid in his direction and she found him studying her with a curiously intent look in his eyes.

As if it was the first time he'd seen her.

Awareness shimmered between them, as powerful as it was unexpected, and then he turned back to his patient, leaving Lara to cope with a frantically pumping heart and shaky knees.

It would have been hard to guess who, out of the two of them, was more shocked.

She didn't gaze at married men.

And even if he wasn't married, she still wouldn't be interested. She had no interest in a relationship at this point in her life.

Ellen was concentrating her attention on Christian again. 'So is that it, then? I see a cardiologist now?'

'That's right.' His voice suddenly clipped, Christian picked up her chart and started to move away from the trolley, but she caught his arm.

'Let me give you my number. If you're at a loose end over Christmas, you can call me. I hate the festive season. You and I could console each other.'

Give the man a bodyguard, Lara thought wearily as Christian carefully extricated himself from Ellen's grip.

'I have your number on the notes in the event that the hospital needs to contact you about something,' he said smoothly, and Ellen's laugh was resigned.

'You're giving me the brush-off, but I suppose that was inevitable. Are you married? Well, of course you're married, the truly gorgeous ones always are. Oh, well, my loss, handsome.'

Christian stilled and Lara held her breath, wondering if he was going to finally lose his cool and say something cutting. Or perhaps he'd produce a picture of his stunning wife and Ellen would spend the rest of Christmas feeling nauseated with jealousy. *And it would be no more than she deserved for being so pushy.* Just because the guy looked like a sex god, it didn't mean he had to be harassed.

But Christian said nothing. In fact, the only suggestion that he'd even heard the question was the faint flicker of a muscle in his jaw. He lowered his head, scribbled something onto the chart and placed it with the rest of the notes. 'The cardiologist is on his way down,' he said evenly, as if he hadn't just been propositioned by a patient. 'He's an excellent doctor and he'll be more than happy to answer all the questions you have about your condition. Staff Nurse King? Nice job.' He studied her for a moment longer than was necessary. 'It's your half-day, isn't it? You should have gone home an hour ago.'

How did he know it was her half-day?

Astonished, Lara watched as he strode out of the room with a firm, confident stride.

He was Christian, the consultant. Christian, the doctor.

He never allowed the smallest glimpse of Christian, the man.

Which was probably why she hadn't bothered looking for flaws.

CHAPTER TWO

'ARE you excited, Daddy? Are you?'

Christian glanced down into the shining eyes of his seven-year-old daughter. *Excited?* 'I'm extremely pleased that you're so happy,' he drawled softly, and she slid her hand into his.

'*I'm* excited. This is the best day of my life. Will it be our turn soon? Will it? We've been waiting for *ages*. Do you think Father Christmas too busy to see us? Are we going to have to come back another time?' Aggie was wearing a bright pink coat with matching gloves and her whole face was a smile as she chattered non-stop. The sound of a choir singing Christmas carols blared and crackled through loudspeakers and the dull ache in Christian's head threatened to turn into a ghastly throb.

The morning had been hideously busy, and prising himself away from the department for a few hours had proved even harder than he'd anticipated.

'He's not too busy to see you, but there are lots of children waiting.' He reached out with his free hand and gently stroked her blonde curls while he glanced along the queue, looking to see if he could track down one of the 'fairies' employed to occupy the children with small toys and sweets while they were waiting. He glanced at his older daughter, who was gazing into space. 'You're quiet, Chloe. Are you all right?'

She sent him a quick smile. 'I'm fine, Daddy. Thanks.'

He looked at her, trying to work out the immediate problem. And there *was* a problem, he knew there was. He gritted his teeth. Until he'd had daughters, he'd thought he'd known a lot about women. 'Is twelve too old to be seeing Father Christmas?'

Was he supposed to know these things?

Colour seeped into her cheeks. 'It's fine, Daddy.'

'She *has* to see Father Christmas,' Aggie announced, hopping from one leg to the other, 'otherwise how is he ever going to know what she wants more than anything in the world?'

Chloe's eyes slid to her sister. 'Father Christmas can't give you everything you want. He isn't a miracle worker.'

'Yes, he is. Try asking and see.'

Had he ever been that innocent or that optimistic?

Wondering whether it was age or life that had turned him into a cynic, Christian studied his eldest daughter's tense profile. She stood quietly in the queue, a far-away look in her eyes. Her cheeks were pale and the skin beneath her eyes was shadowed, as if she wasn't sleeping well. And she was far too quiet, as she so often was these days.

Tension ripped through him.

Could he have changed things? Could he have done things differently?

'Have you made a list? I've made my list.' Aggie danced on the spot, her hand curled tightly around the piece of paper she'd been clutching since he'd collected her from school.

'It's a bit long but I've been good this year.' She peeped cautiously up at her father. 'Sort of…a lot of the time…'

Christian lifted an eyebrow. 'You mean, if I ignore the flooded bathroom, the fire in the kitchen and the ketchup stains on your bedroom carpet?'

'They were *accidents*.'

'I know they were accidents.' And he'd been working. He shuddered when he thought how much worse the 'accidents' could have been. 'It doesn't matter, sweetheart.'

'It wasn't exactly my fault, was it?' Aggie frowned. 'She should have been keeping an eye on me. Nanny TV.'

'Nanny asleep-on-the-sofa,' Chloe murmured, and Christian felt the tension increase dramatically.

Nanny TV. It was only after his daughters had started using that nickname that he'd realised just what the nanny had been doing all day. And it hadn't been looking after his children.

'She's gone,' he said grimly, a flash of anger exploding through his body. 'The new nanny starts tomorrow.'

'Another nanny?' Aggie glanced at her sister. 'What if she doesn't like us?'

'Of course she'll like you.' Christian frowned. 'All nannies like children. That's why they're nannies.'

'Nanny TV didn't like children. She told me that I was more trouble than I was worth.' Aggie smoothed her coat. 'Do we have to have another nanny? We're at school all day. Can't we just come home with you in the evening?'

Chloe shook her head. 'You know we can't do that. Daddy has to work. He has a very important job. He can't always leave at the same time every day. And then there are the nights and the holidays and all the things to be done around the house, like picking up the clothes you drop everywhere.'

Christian let out a long breath. 'Chloe's right, sweet-heart. And, at the moment, my work is very busy.' He didn't even want to think about it. Even taking two hours off to take his daughters to see Father Christmas pricked at his conscience. His colleagues in the emergency depart-ment would be stretched to breaking point. But there was no way he was disappointing his children.

They'd had the year from hell.

He glanced at his watch again and then at the queue, which just didn't seem to be moving.

Aggie tilted her head to one side. 'Are there lots of broken people at the moment?'

Christian blinked at her description. 'Yes—I suppose so. People have accidents—'

'And you stick them back together again.' Aggie gave an understanding smile. 'I know. I know you're very clever. And you need to work, otherwise we wouldn't have any money. Would we have to go to the workhouse?'

'The workhouse?'

'We're learning about it in history. In Victorian times poor children sometimes went into the workhouse. I hope we don't do that. I really like our new house and I love my bedroom. Will we be able to unpack soon?'

Christian opened his mouth and closed it again. Keeping up with the speed of his daughter's conversation required a decent night's sleep and he hadn't had one of those for months. 'We're not poor, Aggie, and you won't go into the workhouse. Workhouses were abolished a long time ago.'

'What's abolished?'

Chloe hushed her. 'Stop asking questions, Aggie! All you do is ask questions and talk, talk, talk! It's no wonder Nanny TV fell asleep on the sofa. She probably died of ex-haustion, listening to your chatter!'

'It's fine to ask questions,' Christian interjected swiftly, noticing Aggie's lip wobble in response to her sister's rebuke. 'And abolish means to do away with something. And we're not leaving our new house and we'll finish unpacking the boxes as soon as I get a free minute—' He broke off as the queue moved forward a little and then stopped again. His heart sank. 'Aggie, how badly do you want to see Father Christmas?'

Aggie beamed. 'More than anything. I think this is the happiest, most exciting day of my life. Thank you, Daddy, for bringing me here. It's my dream.'

No chance of leaving, then, Christian thought wryly as he discreetly checked his watch. He cast a look at Chloe, worried about how quiet she was.

She intercepted his concerned glance and gave a brave smile. 'It's OK, Dad,' she said in a faltering voice. 'Everything is going to be OK. Our new house is lovely. We're all going to have a great Christmas. As soon as I've broken up from school, I can start on those boxes. If Aggie would just stop talking for five minutes and help me, we'll get it done really quickly.'

'You're amazing, do you know that?' Unfailingly impressed by his daughter's resilience, Christian reached for her hand and gave it a squeeze. 'What do you want from Father Christmas, sweetheart?'

He would have given a lot to know, but Chloe didn't reveal her feelings.

Did she talk to her friends?

He almost laughed. Who was he to criticise? He didn't talk to anyone, either.

She looked at him now, her gaze clear and direct. 'I want you to be happy again. I want you to have fun,' she softly. 'That's what I want more than anything.'

Fun? Fun for himself wasn't a priority. All he wanted was to see his daughters relaxed and happy. 'I'm happy, Chlo. I've just been incredibly busy…'

Chloe nodded. 'I know. It doesn't matter. We're doing fine. I know you're busy.'

Too busy to laugh. Too busy to unpack the boxes in their new home. Too busy to see Father Christmas. *Too busy to give his girls everything they needed.*

Christian gritted his teeth, vowing to somehow make himself less busy.

'It's now!' Aggie jumped up and down like a yo-yo. 'That fairy is waving to us. I think it's our turn.'

Why on earth had she ever thought this would be a good idea?

Still recovering her breath after her mad dash from the hospital, Lara smoothed a hand over the glittering net and tulle that floated around her pink tights. It wasn't that she minded the children. She loved the children. She loved the way they stood almost bursting with excitement as they waited, eyes shining, cheeks still pink from the cold. It was the parents that made her despair. She listened to them in the queue, scolding and snapping as if taking the kids to see Father Christmas was just another chore to be ticked off a long list.

Why did people have children if they found them so irritating?

Or maybe that was just one of the ironies of life. Once you had something, you no longer appreciated its value.

Engulfed by a sudden wave of nostalgia, she tried not to dwell on the fact that this would be the first time in her life that she wouldn't be with her own family for Christmas. Her parents had decided to spend the festive period at their cottage in France and her brother was in Australia with his girlfriend.

And it was no good telling herself that she'd be joining him in a matter of weeks. It still felt wrong, not being with her family for Christmas.

Lara felt a flash of sadness.

Things were changing. Her family was changing. She was the only one who had stayed the same.

Would she ever find a man that she wanted to spend a lifetime with? Would she ever have her own children?

Two would be a nice number. Two little girls, exactly like the ones who were next in the queue. Even at a glance she could see that they were entirely different personalities. The elder was quiet and serious and the other was fizzing like a bottle of lemonade that had been shaken until it was ready to explode.

They were gorgeous.

She watched them for a moment with amusement and then looked at the father.

And froze in panic.

Oh, no, no *no!*

It was Christian Blake—looking nothing like his usual self, which was why she hadn't immediately recognised him. Only an hour ago he'd been wearing a blue scrub suit and a distant, forbidding expression. Now there was no sign of the ruthlessly efficient consultant.

This afternoon he was definitely the man and not the doctor.

And an incredibly sexy man.

He'd swapped the scrub suit for a pair of jeans and a chunky sweater that brushed against his strong jaw. His boots looked comfortable and well worn and he wore a long black coat that seemed to emphasise his powerful physique. The younger of the two girls was clinging to his hand and leaping around like a kangaroo on a hot surface.

So not only was he married, he also had two perfect children. And they'd picked this particular day to see Father Christmas.

Pinned to the spot with shock, Lara stifled a whimper. What was she going to do? If her wings had been real, she would have flown up into the rafters and hidden from view.

She wasn't supposed to be here.

But how would she have guessed that a consultant from her department would pick this day to bring his children to visit Santa in his grotto? She'd left him dealing with a patient with a fractured femur. What was he doing here?

Unsure what to do, she waited helplessly for the inevitable recognition. Perhaps her make-up disguised her features; perhaps she looked different in a tutu and tights; perhaps—

'Hello again, Lara.' His eyes—those sharp, sexy blue eyes that never missed anything—slid down her body, lingering on the bodice of her white tutu before sliding over the net and tulle to her shimmering tights.

Her entire body heated under his blatantly masculine scrutiny and Lara wondered which was more embarrassing—being caught moonlighting or being caught moonlighting half-naked. It was a step up from being caught pole-dancing, she thought weakly, but not much.

He dragged his gaze from her legs back to her eyes and they stood for a moment, staring at each other.

Lara opened her mouth to break the tense silence, but no sound came out. Even breathing seemed a challenge.

'Daddy?' The girl in the pink coat tugged at his hand. 'Why are you staring at the fairy?'

Lara clutched at her wand. 'Hi, there.' Her voice sounded strangled. 'I expect your dad is wondering whether I know any good spells. And I wish I did. I could do with a good disappearing spell right now. I don't really

mind who disappears—you or me. Either would be fine.'
Her feeble attempt at humour earned her a raised eyebrow
and a sardonic glance that warned her of trouble.

Panic wrestled with humour and humour won. What
were the chances of a consultant from the emergency department turning up to see Father Christmas in the middle
of his working day?

Seeing the absurdity of it all, Lara started to laugh and
the older girl looked at her with a question in her eyes.

'Why are you laughing?'

Lara's eyes twinkled. 'Because fairies are happy people,' she said huskily, wondering what would happen now.
It was her afternoon off but she knew that her contract
didn't allow her to work elsewhere. Would she lose her job?
She was leaving in a month, of course, but she needed
every last penny she could accumulate.

Merry Christmas, Lara.

The little girl who had been holding Christian's hand
danced forward, her blonde curls bouncing around her
face. 'Is it our turn now? Is he ready for us?'

'He's ready.' Ignoring Christian's intimidating frown,
Lara dropped onto her knees so that she could concentrate
on the child. What was the point in worrying? She couldn't
change the fact that he'd seen her. She may as well get on
with the job, which was to entertain the children. 'What's
your name?'

'Aggie. And this is my big sister, Chloe, and this is my
dad. We're sort of in a hurry because Daddy has to go back
to work.' She leaned forward, her voice a loud whisper.
'My daddy is very clever. He's a doctor and he mends people who break themselves.'

Mends people? Well aware of Christian's skills in the
resuscitation room, Lara decided that it wasn't a bad de-

scription of his job. 'Right…' She cleared her throat. 'In that case, we'd better get you in to see Father Christmas as fast as possible so that your dad can get back to work.'

Aggie reached out a hand and touched her wings. 'Are you a real fairy?'

Lara smiled. 'What do you think?'

'I think you're probably a girl dressed up as a fairy,' Aggie said slowly, 'but you're very pretty.'

'Oh—well—thank you. That's very sweet of you.' For the second time in one day Lara was suddenly aware of Christian's intent masculine appraisal and she blushed and waved a hand. 'Isn't life a weird thing? I go through twenty-five years with no one telling me I look good and suddenly I get told twice in one afternoon. It must be my lucky day. And Father Christmas is waiting. Go on through.' She urged the children forward, intending to follow them, but strong fingers closed around her wrist, preventing her escape.

'And just what,' he demanded in a cool voice, 'is an ED nurse doing dressed up as a fairy in a Christmas grotto? I think some explaining is in order, Staff Nurse King.'

His head was close to hers and she was suddenly engulfed by an explosion of awareness that astonished her. *He's married with two adorable kids*, she reminded herself. What was the matter with her?

Reluctantly, she turned her head to look at him. His blue eyes held hers for a long moment and she felt the strength in her knees vanish. His eyelashes were long and thick and served to accentuate the sensuality of his amazing blue eyes. Strands of dark hair flopped over his forehead, the beginnings of stubble hazed his jaw and he looked nothing like the cool, forbidding consultant she was used to seeing at work.

Someone hand the man a stethoscope, she thought desperately. Anything to remind her who he was.

Lara forced herself to breathe evenly in an attempt to stabilise her churning insides. 'It's my afternoon off,' she croaked, 'and I thought I'd—I'd—'

'Dress as a fairy?'

'I can explain—sort of.'

'You're moonlighting.'

'Not *exactly* moonlighting.'

'You're doing another job. Are you short of money?' One eyebrow lifted in sardonic appraisal. 'Sustaining a gambling habit?'

She giggled at the thought. 'No! I'm saving to go travelling! And I love Christmas,' she confessed. 'I love seeing the children's faces and I don't have any of my own, so I borrow other people's.'

His eyes slid over her body, lingering on the revealing lines of the silky bodice, which she knew was barely decent. Only a few transparent pieces of net and tulle protected her from his scrutiny and she felt her whole body become warm.

Their eyes locked and for a moment neither of them spoke.

The entrance to the grotto felt oppressively hot and suddenly Lara couldn't breathe properly.

'Daddy?' Breathless with excitement, Aggie appeared in the doorway. *'Come on!* It's our turn!'

It took him a moment to answer. 'Yes, sweetheart.' Christian dragged his eyes from Lara's and finally released his iron grip on her wrist. 'Let's see Father Christmas. We can talk about this later.'

'We don't need to,' Lara muttered. 'Honestly, as far as I'm concerned, we can consider the subject closed.'

But the look he shot in her direction indicated that he considered the subject to be far from closed.

Wishing her knees would stop shaking, she led him through to the grotto and laughed aloud at the look of naked incredulity that flickered across his handsome face as he took in the metres of red satin and tinsel and the fake snow. She'd had the same reaction when she'd first seen the interior of the grotto. But the children loved it. Aggie was already sitting next to Father Christmas, her eyes sparkling and her list in her hand.

'Aggie, take your feet off the seat,' Chloe murmured, but her little sister ignored her.

'My feet are clean because these are my absolute bestest shoes.'

Chloe sighed. 'It's "best", not "bestest".'

Aggie ignored her. 'My list is quite long so I hope you're not in a hurry, although it doesn't really matter if you are because I can talk very quickly.' She snuggled a little closer to Father Christmas, her smile wide and her gaze trusting. 'It's not all for me. Some of it's for other people. So I hope I can have a bit more time because I'm doing the talking for three and that's a lot of people. Is that OK with you?'

Father Christmas blinked several times and his mouth twitched under his thick white beard. 'That's fine with me.'

'I have a list here. Do you want to read or shall I just tell you?'

'Aggie, just stop *talking*,' Chloe breathed, folding her arms across her chest and sending a mortified glance towards her father. 'She never stops talking. No one else has a chance of speaking!'

Lara watched the girls and felt envy slide through her body. Christian Blake had a noisy, loving family. Two gorgeous children.

One day, she promised herself. *One day maybe she'd*

*find a man with no flaws and it would be her queuing to
see Father Christmas with her two wonderful children.*

Or four, she thought with humour, if the psychic turned
out to be right. Mindful of the queue building outside, she
stepped forward. 'Let's hear your list, Aggie.'

'OK. Well, I'd really, *really* like a pet but I know I
probably won't get that because Daddy always says that,
if I can't even keep my bedroom tidy, how am I ever going
to clean out a cage?' Aggie peeped at her father hopefully
but the measuring look that Christian gave her in return was
sufficient for Lara to know that pets was a subject that had
been discussed and dismissed on many occasions. 'No pet,
then,' Aggie murmured, subsiding in her seat, 'but if I
really can't have a pet then there are other things…' She
read out a lengthy list, ignoring Chloe's worried glance
towards the clock on the wall. Then she handed the list to
Father Christmas. 'I'll give you this so that you don't have
to remember it all in your head. It's in order, but just to remind you, my best thing would be the bike. And help unpacking the rest of the boxes in my bedroom because since
we moved to our new house I can't find any of my favourite toys, which seems a terrible waste.'

Father Christmas nodded slowly. 'Well, I think I got all
that. What about your big sister? What does she need?'

Chloe flushed. 'Nothing.'

'Go on, Chlo,' Christian urged quietly. 'What do you
want, sweetheart?'

Lara glanced towards him, surprised by the warmth of his
voice. At work in the emergency department he delivered
instructions and commands in a detached, almost cold tone.
He was reassuring to patients when the situation demanded
it, but no one would have described him as touchy-feely. In
fact, some of her colleagues had commented that Christian

Blake was a machine, completely incapable of feeling emotion.

But she knew now that they were wrong.

Christian Blake wasn't incapable of feeling emotion.

'I know what she wants,' Aggie whispered, kneeling up on the seat so that she could whisper in Father Christmas's ear. 'What she wants is for Alex Gregg to ask her to dance at the school disco. Can you fix that?'

'Aggie!' Visibly embarrassed, Chloe turned to her father in horror. 'Can't you stop her talking? All she ever does is talk!'

Aggie's eyes were wide. 'You *do* want that, you know you do! And there's something else.' Undaunted by her sister's quelling look, Aggie smiled happily up at Father Christmas. 'Just one more thing, and it isn't for me.'

Father Christmas stroked his beard. 'Who is it for this time?'

'My dad.'

Christian tensed. 'Aggie, I don't need anything,' he said swiftly. 'And that's enough now. It's someone else's turn to talk to Father Christmas.'

'No. It's *your* turn but I know you won't ask for yourself.' Her chin set at a stubborn angle, Aggie turned back to Father Christmas. 'Daddy needs a new wife. You see, our mummy left us.'

A shocked silence descended on the grotto.

Stunned by that unexpected revelation, Lara couldn't speak or move.

Then Father Christmas cleared his throat. 'She left you?'

'Yes.' Apparently unaware of the tension around her, Aggie continued. 'So now we don't have a mummy and that makes it really hard at home. We have nannies or housekeepers but they're not the same and daddy works so hard in the hospital and that's why we haven't unpacked the boxes yet. What he needs is a miracle. I read about them in a book. A miracle is something amazing that changes everything. If I'm extra-good between now and Christmas, could I have a small miracle?'

Father Christmas appeared to have been struck dumb, so Lara stepped forward, blinking back the tears that had somehow sprung into her eyes.

'The thing about life, Aggie,' she said softly, trying to keep the choke out of her voice, 'is that you never know where the next miracle is going to come from.'

'Well, I don't care where it comes from but I know it has to come *soon*. My friend Katherine at school—her mummy went to heaven and now she has a new mummy but I don't know where she came from. I want to get Daddy a new wife. I want to do an advert like we do for the nannies, but he won't do an advert.'

'She needs to be gagged,' Chloe muttered, shrinking against her father, her expression acutely embarrassed. 'It's the only way. I'm buying her a massive gag for Christmas. And it's not coming off until she learns that silence is golden.'

Christian rubbed a hand over his face and gave a slow shake of his head, clearly struggling to calculate the best way of handling the situation.

'What's gagged?' Aggie looked puzzled, clearly oblivious to the tension that her innocent request had created. 'I just want something nice for Daddy. What's wrong with that?'

Expecting Christian to be furious by his daughter's very frank and public admission, Lara stole a glance in his direction. But she didn't see anger. Instead, she saw concern, gentleness and a touch of sadness. A lump settled in her throat as she watched him step forward and lift his little girl into his arms.

'I don't need a new wife. That isn't the answer.' His voice was soft and he stroked a hand over his little girl's blonde curls. 'And I don't understand why you'd think that, Aggie. We're doing fine, aren't we? What's wrong, sweetheart? What's missing?'

'It's just that I don't want you to be lonely. You need your own special friend,' Aggie whispered, sliding her arms round his neck. 'Chloe has Anna and I have Katherine, but you don't have anyone all for you. If you had a wife, then you'd have someone.'

Christian hesitated. 'It isn't that simple.'

'You mean because of us? Mummy left because of us, didn't she?' Aggie's voice wobbled and she clung to her father like a monkey, her head on his shoulder. 'It's my fault because I talk so much. I do try not to talk but then I sort of want to burst.'

Lara blinked rapidly to try and clear the tears that threatened to obscure her vision. Should she leave the grotto? She knew that Christian Blake was a fiercely private man. He never, ever talked about anything personal. He must be horrified that his little daughter had made such a frank confession in front of a colleague.

But Christian wasn't looking at her. In fact, he didn't even seem aware of her presence. His only interest seemed to be in his little daughter and her feelings.

He hugged her tightly, holding her easily in his arms. 'Aggie, sweetheart, that's enough now. Father Christmas doesn't need to know all the details of our life.'

'Father Christmas doesn't dish out wives and mothers.' Chloe cast a worried glance towards her father and reached forward to grab Aggie. 'I'll take her. Come on, you. We've finished here. We need to go home because Daddy needs to go back to work.'

They posed for the obligatory photograph and then Chloe led Aggie outside.

Lara didn't move.

She didn't know what to do or what to say. She felt as if she'd been eavesdropping on a private conversation. *As though she'd witnessed something that she shouldn't have witnessed.*

She'd assumed he was happily married. Everyone had assumed the same thing. There had been no hints that his private life was in turmoil.

Was he separated or divorced?

What had gone wrong?

'Daddy!' Chloe burst back into the grotto, her blonde hair flying around her face, her tone urgent. 'You have to come *now*! There's a sick girl out here. She was in the queue and then she sort of dropped to the floor and now she's sort of shaking! You have to come!'

CHAPTER THREE

A SICK girl?

Lara glanced at Christian but he was already moving towards the grotto entrance, his response as swift and decisive as it would have been in the emergency department. 'Lara. Come with me. Chloe? Keep an eye on your sister.'

He strode out of the grotto towards the little crowd that had gathered, his black coat swirling around his legs as he walked.

'Someone, help us! Help us!' White with terror, the mother was on her knees by the little girl, trying to lift the child as her little body jerked. 'Olivia? Olivia?' The little girl's body jerked and convulsed beneath her hands and the mother started to sob and scream. 'She's having some sort of fit.'

'Don't hold her. Don't try and restrain her or you might hurt her. I'm a doctor.' Christian dropped to his haunches and put a hand on the mother's shoulder. 'Lara, can you get these people away from here? We don't need an audience.' His voice was sharp and Lara immediately moved everyone back and then dropped to her knees next to him.

'Someone is calling an ambulance.'

'I need something to put underneath her. This floor is hard.' Christian checked the child's airway and swiftly they manoeuvred her into the recovery position.

The store manager hurried up, clutching a soft blanket. 'Is this any use?'

'Perfect.' He slid it under the child's body.

'She's very hot. It must be a febrile convulsion. Being wrapped up in warm layers in this store and standing in the queue, overheating,' Lara murmured, touching the child's forehead and glancing at the mother. 'Has she been ill?'

'She's had a runny nose but nothing too bad, and she was desperate to see Father Christmas. I thought it would distract her.'

'You're right about the warm layers, Lara. We need to try and take some of them off, or at least open them up.' Christian slid the coat from the little girl and opened her cardigan.

'It's freezing outside.' The mother bit her lip. 'I didn't want her to get cold. She kept shivering.'

'She has a temperature,' Lara said gently, 'and it's important that we cool her down. Little children aren't able to control their temperature in the way that adults do. How old is she?'

'Eleven months. I forgot to give her Calpol in the rush to leave the house.'

'Was she drowsy before the seizure?'

'No. Just a bit cross. That's why I thought it would cheer her up to come here. I did the wrong thing. I'm an awful mother.' The mother's face scrunched up and she started to cry. Chloe stepped forward and put a hand on her arm.

'I think you're a lovely mother. What a treat to bring her here. We've just been and it was brilliant. Try not to worry.' Her voice was warm and confident. 'My dad's a doctor and he'll fix it. He's very clever and he always knows what to do when people are ill. Why don't you write her name and age down on a piece of paper because the paramedics will need that when they arrive.'

Lara stared, taken aback by the girl's poise and maturity, but Christian didn't seem surprised. Instead, he glanced across at his elder daughter. 'Chloe—go down to the main entrance and wait for the ambulance. You can tell the paramedics where to come to. It will save time. Tell Aggie to sit still and not run off anywhere.'

'OK, Dad.' Chloe hurried off and Christian turned back to the child.

'The fit has stopped. Has this ever happened before?'

The mother finished scribbling on a piece of paper and shook her head. 'Never.'

'I think the fit was caused by her high temperature. Given that it's the first time she's responded in that way, it's best if we take her to hospital to check her over. You say that she's had a cold. Anything else? Ear infection? Bad throat? Off her food?'

'None of those things. She was a bit fractious yesterday and then last night her temperature went up. But she's been talking about Father Christmas all week and I thought she'd be fine.'

'Let's strip her down to her vest and nappy,' Christian glanced up as the paramedics arrived with Chloe. 'Hi, there, Jack.'

'Dr Blake.' The paramedic flashed him a friendly smile and put his bag down on the floor next to them. 'I thought you were at the hospital today. Sneaking off to see Father Christmas?'

'You know me.' Christian gave a wry smile. 'Can't keep away.' Now that the convulsion had stopped, he quickly examined the little girl. 'This looks like a febrile convul-

sion, Jack. We'll take her in, just so that the paeds can
check her over properly and keep an eye on her for a while.'

'Right. That girl of yours told us what to expect. She's
a cracker is your Chloe.'

'This child needs to go into the unit. I've got no equipment with me so I can't examine her properly and, anyway,
she's better off in hospital if this is her first febrile convulsion. Lara, can you call Paeds and warn them?' He pulled
a mobile phone out of his pocket and handed it to her while
the paramedic looked on in surprise.

'Lara! I didn't recognise you.' His gaze was startled.
'What—? I mean, why—?'

'Don't ask,' Christian advised dryly, checking the child's
pulse rate again. 'She's coming round. She will be drowsy
for a while,' he warned the mother and she gave a nod.

'Will they do loads of tests?' Her voice was a whisper
and she looked shocked and terrified as her little girl was
lifted onto the trolley. 'Could she have meningitis or something? You read about it all the time and it terrifies me.'

'She isn't showing any signs of meningitis but she'll
be checked properly by a paediatrician when she gets to
the hospital.'

Lara spoke to the paediatrician at the hospital and then
handed the phone back to Christian. 'They're expecting her.'

'Good.' He rose to his feet and slipped the phone back
into his pocket while Lara stood there, wanting to help but
not knowing how best to do it.

'I can go in the ambulance with her if you like. You need
to get your girls home.'

'You'd risk walking into the emergency department
dressed like a fairy? You'd never live it down.'

Lara smiled. 'It's fine. If anyone teases me, I can just
turn them into a frog with my wand.'

'We'll take it from here,' Jack said cheerfully. 'We'll see you back at the hospital.'

The paramedics left with the sick child and the mother, and the crowd that had gathered around them gradually dispersed.

Lara glanced across the room towards his children. Chloe was holding onto Aggie's hand. 'You have wonderful children, Dr Blake.'

'Yes.' He looked at them for a moment and then stirred. 'I need to get back to the department. You know how busy it is at the moment.'

'Do you want me to come in to work? Take the girls home for you? There must be something I can do.' She wanted to do something. *Wanted to say something.* But they were standing in a busy department store, surrounded by Christmas shoppers.

Christian's expression was guarded. 'I don't need help,' he said quietly, 'and I can take care of my girls.'

'I'm sure you can. But who takes care of you, Christian?' The words flew from her mouth before she could stop them and he lifted an eyebrow.

'I think I'm probably old enough to take care of myself.'

She flushed. 'Everyone needs to be loved. Oh, God, I'm starting to sound like my mother. I'm just saying that you need to be looked after, too. Not that I'm trying to suggest that I…' Her colour deepened as she realised how her words had sounded. 'I didn't exactly mean that I—'

'Staff Nurse King.' His voice was soft and the expression in his eyes was remote and discouraging. 'Take my advice and quit now before you say anything else that you don't mean.'

She held his gaze and awareness flared between them. The atmosphere crackled with tension and this time she was unable to defuse it by telling herself that he was married. 'I could help you. I'd like to help,' she said impulsively, and he was silent for a long moment, as if he didn't know quite how to respond to her offer.

Finally he drew breath. 'I'll pretend we didn't just have this conversation.' He stepped back from her. 'And I'll pretend that I didn't see you dressed as a fairy. If the chief executive decides to bring his grandchildren to see Father Christmas, I advise you to use those wings of yours and fly off somewhere where he can't see you. I'll see you back in the emergency department.'

The weather grew suddenly cold and the next week was horribly busy.

A week after her encounter with Christian in the grotto, Lara was doing a dressing in the treatment room when Jane stuck her head round the door. 'Christian wants you in Resus, Lara.' She gave an apologetic smile. 'Listen to me! If I had a pound for every time I utter that phrase, I could retire somewhere hot and spend my life lying under a palm tree. I pointed out that there are actually other nurses in this department but apparently you're the sharpest. It's going to be awful when you leave. The rest of us will have to wake up and do some work.'

Lara wasn't listening. Instead, she was trying to produce a reasonable explanation for the fact that her hands were shaking at the mere mention of Christian's name. The meeting in Santa's grotto had changed their relationship. *For her, at least.* She no longer saw Christian Blake as the slightly intimidating senior consultant, remote and out of reach. Married. Instead, she saw him as a warm, caring father. *An incredibly sexy, single man...*

Oh, for crying out loud, what was the matter with her?

It didn't matter if he was single and sexy. She was going to Australia.

And that was why she was thinking about him, of course.

Because she wasn't in a position to begin a relationship with anyone and you always wanted what you couldn't have.

Feeling the familiar rush of excitement at the thought of her proposed trip, she rationalised her feelings by reminding herself that the unobtainable was always more alluring.

Lara finished with the patient, washed her hands and followed Jane out into the corridor.

'So what have we got this time?'

'Twenty-five-year-old female cyclist hit black ice and collided with a car. She'd just had the office Christmas lunch so I think there might have been some alcohol involved. The ambulance is due in five minutes. But Christian wants you in there. Apparently you're the most efficient nurse he's ever worked with.' Jane shrugged. 'All I can say is the guy must have worked with some real duds.'

Lara laughed. 'Thanks, boss. You're a real boost to my confidence.'

She followed Jane into Resus, confident that her mind was back on the job. One swift glance towards Christian told her that he was well and truly back in his role of consultant—driven, confident and decisive.

No problem. Everything was fine.

And then he looked at her.

He was in conversation with the radiologist but his gaze settled on Lara and for a brief moment their eyes held and something passed between them—a wordless communication that made her body flare hot with awareness.

Christian didn't falter in his instructions to the radiologist but Lara felt her mind go blank and for a brief, terrifying moment she couldn't concentrate on a thing. She saw his eyes darken slightly and knew that he felt it, too. And sensed that the unexpected chemistry somehow irritated him.

Aware that her knees and hands were shaking, she bit back a whimper of frustration and turned her back on him, forcing herself to cut the connection.

What was the matter with her?

It normally took her less than five minutes to start spotting all the things that were wrong with a man.

Why wasn't she doing that with Christian?

She needed to concentrate harder. He probably had millions of flaws, it was just that she hadn't been looking properly.

Gritting her teeth, she reached for the equipment that was mandatory for dealing with trauma patients. Swiftly she sorted out a gown, gloves and eye protection, all the time reminding herself that Christian Blake might be a hotshot in the resuscitation room, a fabulous father and indecently good-looking, but that didn't mean that he was perfect.

The trauma team was assembling, each member occupied with preparing for the arrival of the patient.

Christian was prowling around the room, checking that everything was in place and that everyone understood their responsibilities. 'Jane? Have you bleeped the trauma consultant?'

'He's on his way.'

The trauma registrar hurried into the room and then the doors to Resus flew open again and the paramedics surged into the room with the patient on a stretcher and ED staff alongside.

Everyone moved swiftly into position, carefully transferring the patient but maintaining silence while the paramedics described the mechanism of injury, the patient's signs and what treatment had been given.

Christian's gaze flickered to the whiteboard at the head of the trolley, which had already been covered in black, scrawling notes by the person who had taken the call from Ambulance Control.

Another doctor moved to the head of the trolley to clear and secure the airway and Lara reached for a pair of more robust gloves so that she could help remove the patient's clothes.

How did Christian do it?

How did he hold down such a busy job and look after two lively daughters on his own?

But she knew the answer to that, of course, thanks to Aggie's innocent declaration. He was living in a house with boxes still unpacked and he relied on nannies. He was doing the job and being a father to his children, but not much else.

By now the patient's airway was secure, the clothes had been removed from the patient's body and two peripheral lines were in place. The radiographer had moved the X-ray machine into position on the patient's left side and someone pulled a unit of O-negative blood out of the warmer.

'Chest and AP pelvis to start with,' Christian ordered, 'and then I want to do a FAST test. Her systolic pressure is less than 90 so she's bleeding from somewhere. The question is whether it's just the pelvis. Keep the pelvic splint in place and don't move her around.'

Lara moved the machine closer to the trolley. 'You don't want to send her straight for a laparotomy and packing?'

'I might still do that but I want to see the result of the FAST test first. She's haemodynamically unstable so if it's negative then she's going straight to the angio suite for embolisation.'

He was examining the patient's chest now, checking for signs of life-threatening thoracic conditions. 'She has a seatbelt mark on her chest. But her lungs seem clear and there's no evidence of tension pneumothorax or haemothorax.'

'You're not going to spring the iliac crests?' Penny, one of the casualty officers, asked the question and Lara frowned.

Christian glanced in her direction and gave a faint smile. 'I think Staff Nurse King has the answer to that question.'

'Her veins and arteries are trying to clot,' Lara said immediately, wondering whether Penny ever bothered to read a textbook or a medical journal. Despite four months in the ED, she had yet to make much of a favourable impression. 'If you spring the iliac crests, you risk disturbing the clot and increasing the bleeding.'

'Lara is right.' Christian dragged the ultrasound machine closer to the patient. 'Protect the clot. No springing. No log-rolling. I don't need to tell you how serious an unstable pelvic fracture can be.'

Lara's eyes were on the machine. 'Her blood pressure is dropping.'

'Give her another unit of warmed blood through the rapid infuser.' Christian was still checking the patient. 'Are those blood results back yet? If we just pour fluid into her, she'll have coagulation problems. Now, let's have a look at her abdomen. I want to know if there's any intraperitoneal bleeding. Jane, can you ring through to the angio suite and fill them in? I have a feeling we're going to need their help and it takes them a while to set up.'

'Will do.' Jane hurried over to the phone and Lara stepped a little closer so that she could watch Christian do the FAST test.

He placed the transducer on the patient's abdomen, just above the pubic bone, and studied the screen, a frown on his face. 'Penny? You can't see from over there—come closer. I'm looking for free intraperitoneal fluid—fluid collects in the pouch of Douglas and you can visualise that with the scan.' He paused for a moment, staring at the screen with total concentration. 'It's negative but that doesn't exclude intra-abdominal injury.'

The anaesthetist adjusted the oxygen flow and glanced at the monitor. 'They don't like having patients this unstable in the angio suite, Christian. It's not a good place to resuscitate a patient.'

'Interventional angio is the best way to stop the bleeding.' Cool and unflustered, Christian checked a set of blood results and shook his head. 'Give her FFP and cryoprecipitate. Let's take a look at that X-ray, Maria.'

'I have it here.'

He studied the screen. 'Well, that's fairly obvious, isn't it? Penny? Take a look at this X-ray.'

Lara recorded the patient's observations again and glanced towards the screen, hoping that Penny would spot whatever it was she was supposed to spot.

The girl needed a boost to her confidence.

'She has an antero-posterior compression fracture.' Penny leaned closer to the screen and touched it with her finger. 'It's causing separation of the pubic symphysis and widening of both sacroiliac joints.'

Lara breathed a sigh of relief and slipped her pen back into her pocket.

'Well done.' Christian nodded. 'Also known as an "open-book" fracture. Significant opening of the sacroiliac joints is associated with tearing of the major blood vessels that overlie the joint. So what we're looking at here is potential for serious vascular damage.'

'And major blood loss.' Lara grimaced as she looked at the blood-pressure reading. 'Christian?'

'I've seen it.'

Penny frowned. 'But the X-ray doesn't look that bad.'

Lara handed Christian a set of results. 'With every pelvic fracture it's important to think about the mechanism of injury because the damage on the X-ray may not actually reflect the degree to which the bones were separated during the actual injury. So you need to be alert for major soft-tissue damage.'

Christian scanned the results. 'I want to take her straight to angio. Everything else can wait.'

Derek adjusted the oxygen. 'You don't want to examine her back?'

'That can wait, too. I don't want to risk dislodging the clot in her pelvis.'

Lara watched him, envying the ease and confidence with which he tackled every case that came his way. In two months, working alongside him in the ED, she'd never seen him remotely rattled and she loved working with him.

'Penny, what do you know about interventional radiology?'

'Very little,' the junior doctor admitted frankly, and he gave a nod.

'Perhaps you should go along and observe.'

'Oh, yes, please.' She nodded immediately and then fell silent as one of the nurses drew his attention to the monitor.

'Her blood pressure is dropping into her boots.'

They worked swiftly, using the rapid infuser to push blood into the critically ill patient.

'Her pressure is coming up a little.' Christian looked at Lara. 'Let's do another FAST test, just in case things have changed.'

He performed the test, satisfied himself that interventional angiography offered the best chance for the patient and the team transferred her to the angio suite.

Left alone in Resus, Lara started clearing up and re-stocking, ready for the next patient.

She worked methodically, following the agreed protocol, and she had just started on the intubation tray when Christian came back into the room. She glanced at him expectantly. 'How's our patient doing?'

'Well, she didn't die in the corridor, if that's what you're asking me.' His eyes were tired. 'It's too soon to say. Can I ask you a question?'

'Of course.' She picked up a laryngoscope and snapped it open, checking the bulb. 'Ask away.'

'Why didn't you do medicine? You're easily the brightest nurse I've ever worked with.'

'You think nursing is a career for those too thick to become doctors?' Lara's eyes twinkled. 'Be careful where you voice that opinion, Dr Blake. You might just find yourself with a compound orbital fracture.'

'You're threatening to black my eye?' He strolled into the room. 'I never would have suspected that you have such a violent nature. For the record, that wasn't what I was suggesting. Obviously nursing is a distinct career choice. The reason I wondered about you is because you're so obviously interested in the diagnostic side of things.'

'I'm not sure that I am.' Lara wrinkled her nose thoughtfully. 'I think I probably just have a naturally interfering nature. And a big mouth. If I think I know what's going on, I have to speak up.'

'Did you consider becoming a doctor?'

'No, not really. I suppose I'm more interested in the person than the disease.' She smiled. 'And I'm not serious enough to be a doctor. I'd crack a joke at the wrong moment.'

'You're serious enough when you need to be.'

She found his gaze distinctly unsettling. 'I don't have the necessary cool to do the job you do. When you're with a patient, you're very emotionally detached.'

'My job is to deal with the immediate physical trauma.'

'And you do it brilliantly. You're a clever man, Dr Blake.' She put the laryngoscope back on the tray, trying to understand the sudden tension in the atmosphere. They were just colleagues—nothing more. 'So you should be relieved that you didn't try and see Father Christmas in his grotto yesterday, because the queues were enough to make a grown man sob. How are your girls?'

He hesitated, as if he wasn't entirely comfortable with the topic of conversation. 'Excited about Christmas. We have a new nanny installed in our house so hopefully a few of those boxes might get unpacked soon.'

His oblique reference to Aggie's impulsive confession in the grotto made her wonder if he was concerned about his privacy.

'Listen, Christian, I hope you don't feel awkward about last week. A little girl's chat with Father Christmas should always be kept private. Just in case you're worrying, I never repeat anything I hear in the grotto.'

He watched her. 'I'm not worrying. It's hard to keep anything private with Aggie around, as you've probably gathered.'

'She's adorable. You're so lucky.' Faint colour touched her cheeks. 'Sorry. I mean, it's obviously a very difficult time for you and—'

'I know I'm lucky, Lara,' he said softly. 'I love my girls.'

'Yes, that's obvious.' She gave a wistful sigh and then smiled at him. 'It must be hard, moving house just before Christmas.'

'We moved three months ago, just before I started this

job. But with the demands of a new job and the endless nightmare of nannies, I haven't had time to finish unpacking the boxes.' He gave a self-deprecating smile. 'But clearly it has to be a priority now that emptying boxes is on Aggie's Christmas list.'

'And what's on your Christmas list, Dr Blake?'

'Top of my list is a decent nanny. The current one has turned up to work five days in succession so that's a start. If she turns out to be Mary Poppins then I'm going to have a happy Christmas.'

'That doesn't seem like a very exciting Christmas present for you.'

He studied her face for a long moment. 'I don't need exciting. What I need is to not worry about my children when I'm working.'

'Yes. I can see that must be a worry. In fact, the whole thing must be a worry. 'Do you know what you need, Christian?'

'What's that?'

'Fun.' She tilted her head and looked at him with laughter in her eyes. 'You look like a man who is taking life much too seriously at the moment. What you need is fun.'

CHAPTER FOUR

Fun?

Why was everyone suddenly so obsessed with him having fun?

First Chloe, now Lara. Only, coming from Lara, the word *fun* took on an entirely different meaning.

When Chloe had used the word, he'd immediately thought of rowdy games of catch in the park, sledging in the snow on Hampstead Heath, playing Monopoly in front of the fire, with Aggie cheating. When Lara had used it, entirely different images had filled his brain.

Dangerous images.

He remembered her legs in the fairy costume, long and slim, her body slender but with curves in all the right places.

She was getting under his skin, Christian thought grimly, struggling against the hot burn of lust that threatened to devour him.

It wasn't going to happen.

His girls had been through hell and they'd only just started to show signs of settling down. There was no way he was going to do anything that might threaten their new-found security. They needed life to be stable and predictable. They didn't need their father involved with another woman.

Christian strode back to the comparative sanctuary of his office, wondering what was happening to him. He'd never had any trouble focusing on his work and since the divorce he'd had no trouble in *not* noticing women. But that had changed when he'd moved hospitals and met Lara King.

No man could fail to notice Lara.

She had a vibrant, energetic personality and her sense of humour infected the whole department. And as for the way she looked—well, her appearance matched her personality. Her hair flicked cheekily up at the edges, she wore an almost permanent smile on her face and her deep blue eyes always seemed to be twinkling with humour.

But despite her obvious attractions, he'd managed to think of her only as a talented colleague.

Until a week ago.

Meeting her in the Christmas grotto had changed everything.

His life was no longer neatly and securely divided into work and home. She'd bridged the two and in doing so had forced a hole through the defences he'd built around himself. And it was nothing to do with the fact that Aggie had so innocently broadcast the details of his personal life and everything to do with his awareness of Lara as a woman.

With a soft curse, Christian sprawled in the chair behind his desk, ignoring the fact that his computer was telling him that he had seventy-two new messages in his inbox.

He couldn't stop thinking about her.

She was all energy and laughter but his attempts to dampen his libido by dismissing her as vacuous and lightweight were continually thwarted by the fact that she was, without doubt, the brightest nurse he'd ever worked with. She was always one step ahead of him and her experience in the ED smoothed every clinical situation.

She was vivacious, full of life and almost impossibly sexy and, if she'd come into his life at a different time…

But she hadn't, he reminded himself grimly, gritting his teeth and hitting a key on his computer so that he could view his emails.

And it didn't matter how bright she was or how attractive. It didn't matter how strongly his body reacted to her.

He didn't want any sort of relationship with a woman. It was far too soon.

The girls weren't ready.

And he wasn't ready, either.

The following day Lara was strapping a patient's ankle in the treatment room when Jane put her head round the door.

'Have you seen Christian?'

'Not since lunchtime.' Lara looked up. 'Why?'

'Because his daughter is in Reception, asking to see him.'

'Which one?'

Jane stared at her. 'How many does he have? How do you suddenly know so much about his children?'

'He must have mentioned it,' Lara said casually. 'I'll go and see to the daughter while you find Christian. I've finished here, anyway.' She handed the patient an information sheet. 'Keep the leg up when you're sitting down. You can take some ibuprofen or paracetamol for the pain.'

She washed her hands thoroughly, wondering why one of Christian's girls had suddenly arrived in the emergency department. 'Is she on her own?'

'As far as I could see. I wonder if he's gone down to the chief exec's office or something?' Jane slid out of the room to continue her hunt for Christian and Lara hurried through to Reception.

Aggie sat there, looking forlorn. Her arm was bandaged and her face was covered in spots.

'Oh, my goodness, what's happened to you?!' Lara swiftly entered the code that unlocked the door through to Reception and hurried over to the little girl. 'Aggie. Do you remember me?'

'You look like that fairy. But without the wings.' Aggie gave a faltering smile and Lara saw the remains of tears on her cheeks.

'That's me. The fairy. My name's Lara. What's happened? Are you ill? How long have you had spots?' She peered a little closer at Aggie's face and realised that, close up, the spots looked like nothing she'd ever seen before. 'Er…Aggie, about these spots…'

'I need to see Daddy.' Her voice was a soft whisper and Lara nodded.

'Of course you do. But tell me what happened. Why is your wrist bandaged?' She looked at the loose, saggy bandage and knew immediately who had done the bandaging. 'Did you fall?'

Aggie swung her legs. 'Not exactly.'

'And those spots…' Lara reached out a finger and rubbed at the spots. 'Aggie, why have you been painting spots on yourself?'

'Because I need to look ill,' Aggie blurted out. 'Daddy said we weren't to bother him at the hospital unless one of us was ill, but I really, *really* need to talk to him. It's totally urgent and important.'

Lara stood up and held out her hand. 'Come on. Come through and see our toys and I'll find your daddy. Where's Chloe?'

'She's playing with a friend. I was at home with Nanny Bottle. But she was very thirsty so she drank and drank and then her eyes went all funny and her voice sounded jumpy. And then she couldn't make my tea.'

'Nanny Bottle?' Lara tapped in the code and opened the door. 'Is she your new nanny?'

'Yes. She's worse than Nanny TV,' Aggie confided gloomily. 'At least Nanny TV was awake—when she wasn't asleep.'

'Your new nanny is asleep?'

'I expect she was tired from all that drinking. She sort of drank and drank and then swayed like this and hiccoughed a lot.' Aggie demonstrated. 'And then her eyes went funny and her voice went jumpy. And she fell asleep.'

Drunk?

Lara glanced at her in horror as she led her through to Christian's office. 'Don't worry about that now. You'll be safe here. This is your dad's office.'

'I know. He brought me once so that I can imagine where he is if I miss him during the day.' Aggie settled confidently into the chair just as the door opened again and Christian strode in.

'Aggie?'

'Daddy.' There was a hitch in her voice and she shrank back slightly in the chair. 'Promise you're not angry.'

'What are you doing at the hospital? And what's happened to your arm?' He looked at the bandages and his eyes narrowed as he studied the spots. 'Aggie—'

'I tried to make them look real but the colour is wrong and I didn't know what to do,' Aggie burst out. 'You told us not to bother you unless one of us was ill so I thought if I bandaged myself you wouldn't be angry because you'd think I was hurt.'

Christian took a deep breath and dropped onto his haunches, his eyes level with his daughter's. 'I'm not angry with you, sweetheart. But I do want to know what you're doing here. Where's Mrs Birkin? She's supposed to be looking after you.'

Aggie curled her legs under her, rubbing her little shoes on Christian's chair. 'She was thirsty. And now she's lying on the floor.'

'Thirsty?' Christian stared at her for a moment and then his mouth hardened. 'You mean she was drinking? *What* was she drinking?'

'Something from a dark bottle. She must have liked it because she drank *loads*. Then she started talking funny and lay down on the floor. I couldn't get her to talk and I was worried. I thought she'd had an accident.'

'Drinking from a bottle?' His eyes burning with anger, Christian rose to his feet and looked at Lara. 'I need to go home.'

'Of course you do. I'm due to finish in five minutes. Why don't I come with you?' She didn't know what had prompted her to suggest it, and she braced herself for rejection.

He hesitated and then gave a swift nod. 'That would be helpful. You can stay with the children while I sort out the nanny, if that's all right with you.'

'Of course.'

At that moment Chloe came flying through the door. 'Dad! Aggie's not at home and Mrs Birkin is—' Her face cleared as she saw her sister nestled into the chair. 'Oh. Thank goodness. I got home from my friend's and there was no sign of them and Nanny Birkin was asleep.' She looked at Aggie. 'How did you get to the hospital?'

'I called that taxi number that's stuck to the board in the kitchen and told him it was urgent.'

Chloe blinked. 'And where did you find money?'

Aggie shrank back in her chair, her eyes huge. 'Your money-box?'

'Quick thinking,' Christian said smoothly, grabbing his coat and lifting Aggie into his arms. 'We're going home now. Lara is going to come with us.'

'Will she wear her fairy costume? Can we play dressing-up?'

Lara noticed the grim set of Christian's mouth and knew how upset he was. 'Dressing-up is my favourite game,' she said cheerfully. 'Will you do my make-up?'

Christian leaned against the kitchen door with his eyes closed, willing his problems to magically disappear.

In the past two hours he'd sobered up the nanny, fired her and lodged a formal complaint with the agency. Now he just had to work out how to reorganise his life so that he could work and look after his daughters.

'Christian?'

He opened his eyes to find Lara standing in front of him. She'd done such a good job of occupying the children, he'd forgotten that he wasn't alone in the house. 'Thank you for keeping them out of the way while I dealt with that.' His eyes slid over her. She was wearing a tiara and there were two large scarlet streaks on her cheeks. 'What happened to you?'

She grinned. 'Aggie happened to me. We're playing princesses. Which involves lots of make-up. If you think this is bad, you should see what she did to Chloe. I'll say this for her, your elder daughter is very long-suffering.'

He eyed the red streaks on her face. 'You look as though you need a maxillary facial surgeon.'

'That's just the blusher she used. Apparently princesses always have rosy cheeks.' She glanced around her and he saw her looking at the boxes.

'I was hoping that the nanny would help to unpack the last of the boxes,' he said, wondering why he was explaining himself to her. *What did it matter what she thought?* 'I've only done the important ones.'

'You did Aggie's bedroom. It's so pretty. Like a fairy grotto.'

'She loves everything pink, as I'm sure you noticed, and I wanted her to feel at home as quickly as possible. I should have done Chloe's, too, but she's older and…' He shrugged, wondering with a pang of guilt whether he'd been neglecting his elder daughter. 'Chloe never complains.'

'She's a sweet-natured girl.' Lara reached out and touched his arm, her expression concerned. 'Are you all right? You haven't had the best day.'

Her touch seemed to connect with every nerve ending in his body and he tensed, battling with an astonishingly powerful desire to haul her against him and bring his mouth down on hers. He was entirely confident that a couple of hours naked with Lara would make his problems considerably less important.

But that wasn't an option.

Reminding himself that he was a father with responsibilities, one of which was not indulging his own fantasies, he took a step back from her, wishing he hadn't noticed the thickness of her lashes and the softness of her mouth.

A vision of her in her fairy costume sprang into his head and he ran a hand over the back of his neck and prowled across the kitchen, putting some distance between them. With a considerable effort, he turned his mind back to the reality of his life. 'She was drunk, Lara.'

'I know.'

He turned to face her, a surge of helpless anger engulfing his attempt at calm. 'I left my children with a drunk.'

'No, you didn't. You left your children with a nanny recommended by a reputable agency.' Lara's voice was steady. 'If anyone is to blame, it's them.'

'Maybe. I still feel responsible. It means more change and upheaval for the girls and they've already had enough. I won't be using that agency again, that's for sure. Which gives me a problem because none of the other agencies have anyone available right now. Apparently no one changes jobs three weeks from Christmas. Aggie's right. What we need around here is a miracle.'

Deeply worried about his children, he paced across to the window and stared across the huge garden that stretched behind the house. Snow was fluttering down from a grey, wintry sky, settling on the grass like icing sugar, and the holly tree was crowded with bright red berries. The house was beautiful. It was just a shame that he hadn't had time to turn it into a home. 'I need to get on the phone and call every agency in London. But I keep thinking that I don't want to leave them with anyone.' *That had never been what he wanted for his children.* 'If Aggie hadn't shown such common sense…' He broke off, still dealing with the enormity of what could have happened to his girls.

'But she did. And that's reassuring, isn't it? Despite her age, she's obviously very sensible and practical. That must make you very proud of her. Of both of them. They're gorgeous children.'

'And they deserve better than this. They've been through hell and they need stability.'

'I have a solution. I should have thought of it a week ago when I first saw you in the grotto. I can do it.'

'You can do what?'

'Help you with the girls.'

For a moment Christian just stared at her, wondering if he'd heard her correctly. 'You already work as a nurse in the busiest emergency department in the capital, and on the side you're a fairy. How many jobs does one woman need?'

'I could do it, no problem. I'd just move in with you and then I'd be here in the mornings and the evenings.'

Move in?

Christian froze, his tension levels soaring. He was about to utter a curt rejection of her idea when she looked up at him and smiled. He felt himself instantly drawn into the warmth of that smile, even though the cynical side of him—*the side that was experienced with women*—was shouting a loud warning.

She was like a siren, he thought, *drawing a man onto the rocks.*

But even that knowledge didn't stop him noticing that her eyes were actually more violet than blue and that her blonde hair was still flicking up slightly at the ends, giving her appearance an elfin quality that was astonishingly appealing.

'Christian?' She looking at him with amusement in her eyes and he suddenly remembered that he was supposed to be responding to her proposal.

'No.' *He didn't need a sexy woman living in his house.* 'Definitely not.'

'It would only be over the Christmas period. Why would you say no?' She looked slightly baffled, as if the possibility of rejection hadn't occurred to her. 'I'm the answer to your prayers.'

He gritted his teeth and reined in his libido. 'Lara, you're *not* the answer to my prayers.'

Her merry smile faltered and the dimple threatened to disappear. 'You don't trust me with your children?'

'This has nothing to do with the children.'

'Well, of course it does!' She stared at him in astonishment. 'It has everything to do with the children. That's why I'm offering. What else are we talking about here?'

He lifted an eyebrow. *Did she need him to spell it out?*

She stared at him for a moment and then her eyes narrowed. 'Ah. I see. You think I've just made an indecent proposition. I've noticed that women seem to do that when they're around you. It must get pretty awkward.'

'Occasionally.' He ran a hand over the back of his neck, struggling to be tactful. 'Thanks for your offer, but—'

'Christian.' She lifted a hand to interrupt him. 'Stop now, before you say something that will make this embarrassing. Firstly, I wasn't making an indecent proposal. It was a genuine offer to help with the children. Secondly, although you are *indecently* handsome, I don't have designs on you. You're quite safe.'

'Safe?'

'Yes.' Her eyes sparkled with humour. 'I admit that I find you very attractive. And I like you. A lot.'

'Lara!'

'What's the matter now?'

He inhaled sharply and took a step back to prevent himself from reaching for her. 'I'm not in a position to indulge in a relationship,' he said tersely, deciding that, if she was going to be honest, then he may as well be, too.

'Neither am I. That's what I'm trying to tell you. I'm hopeless at relationships. *Useless.* Ask my mother if you don't believe me. For the past four years, my longest relationship has been three dates.' She held up her fingers to emphasise her point. '*Three*. Not impressive, by anyone's standards.'

'Three dates?' He studied her pretty face with something approaching disbelief. 'I find that hard to believe.'

'So does my mother. She can't believe that I haven't managed to find Mr Right when I'm living in a city with a huge population of single men. I'm obviously doing something horribly wrong. But, anyway, what I'm trying to say is that, if you don't want a relationship, then I'm your woman.'

'That sounds like something of a contradiction.'

'Yes, you're right. It does.' Her eyes brimmed with laughter and the dimple was back in the corner of her mouth. 'But you know what I mean.'

Christian refused to allow himself to look at the dimple. 'I'm not sure that I do. Lara, it's impossible.' *He didn't trust himself.* 'No.'

'If you say no, you'll regret it.'

'I'm saying no and I'm not going to regret it.' Against his will, his eyes dropped to her mouth and his entire body throbbed with sexual tension. 'It's a wild, crazy idea.'

'You're just hesitating because of this whole stupid chemistry thing. But you don't need to worry. It's the perfect solution, Christian. I'm on the early shift right up until Christmas so I can pick up the girls from school and take them home.'

'They're on holiday for the four days before Christmas.' *What was he saying?* What did it matter when they were on holiday? He should have been saying no and pushing her out of the door.

She shrugged. 'We can mix and match our days off.'

There was a long, pulsating silence and he stared down at her. 'Why would you make that offer?' He was experienced enough with women to be wary.

'Honestly? Company.' She hesitated and then gave a twisted little smile. 'This is going to be the first year ever that my family won't be together at Christmas and I'm staying in London. Pathetic, isn't it? I'm twenty-five and I'm really sad that I'm not going home for Christmas.'

'You obviously have a close family.' *Which made her lucky, not pathetic.*

'Yes. Well, if I moved in with you, I could still have a family Christmas.'

He felt himself wavering and tried to talk some sense into himself. It was a ridiculous suggestion. 'Apart from the trip to the grotto, I haven't thought about Christmas.'

'Aggie's thinking about it. She gave Santa a very long list. Someone needs to start shopping and unpacking boxes.'

'I know.' Christian ran a hand over his face, feeling trapped. 'It's a generous offer but…no. I have to say no, Lara.'

She studied him for a moment. 'I'm going to be frank here. You don't want a relationship, neither do I. Just in case you don't believe me and you're worried that I might be difficult to shift, you ought to know that my flight to Sydney is on the 15th of January, and that isn't changing.'

'You're going to Sydney?'

'Yes. I'm visiting my brother and his girlfriend in Australia. And I'll probably do a bit of travelling. So, you see, there isn't a problem because I'm leaving the country. How much safer do you need to feel? Christian, I can help you, I know I can. I can unpack the boxes in the house, I can put up Christmas decorations, I can organise you a big, happy family Christmas. And as for the chemistry…' She waved a hand dismissively. 'We'll ignore it.'

Was that possible?

'You've resigned from your job?'

'Yes.'

Why did he care? 'You seriously expect me to believe that you want to move in with two demanding children, a grouchy guy who hasn't even had time to unpack the boxes from his house move and cook Christmas dinner?' His voice was rougher than he'd intended. 'It's most women's idea of hell.' *It had certainly been his wife's idea of hell.*

'Not mine.' She stuffed her hands into the pockets of her jeans. 'Look, London is horrifically expensive for a nurse and my flat is tiny. On Christmas Day, it's going to be me or the turkey. There's certainly not room for both of us.' The laughter brimming in her eyes brought a smile to his lips.

'You wouldn't bother cooking a turkey for one.'

'You're right. So lunch would probably be a cranberry omelette. Which makes my Christmas all the more pitiful. Take pity on me and give me the run of your beautiful kitchen. I could do amazingly creative things with your range cooker.'

'It's not your cooking that worries me.'

'What, then?'

'The children could get attached to you.'

'Not in the space of a few weeks. We'll just have some fun. I'm sure it will be fine if we're just honest with them. We'll just tell the girls right from the start that it's only temporary. I'm leaving in less than a month from now so they can't get too attached. I mean, they haven't exactly mourned any of their nannies, have they? I'm just the woman who collects them from school, helps them with homework and cooks their tea. It will be too short term for them to grow too fond of me. I'm just here to make Christmas easier. It's always a busy time of year. If you haven't had time to unpack boxes, when are you going to find time to shop for the girls and decorate a tree?'

It was a completely ridiculous offer. He was experienced enough with women to know that the chemistry between them was astonishingly powerful.

Was it really something that they'd be able to ignore?

'It's Christmas,' Lara said, her tone persuasive. 'You're not going to find anyone else that you can trust. The girls and I will have fun together and, when you're at home, I'll just hide in my room with my books on the Great Barrier Reef. I won't intrude on your family, I promise.'

Christian looked at her, struggling against a powerful impulse to follow her suggestion, clamp his mouth down on hers and kiss her until she no longer had the breath to speak. *She had an incredibly kissable mouth.* 'My girls are very demanding. They're lively and noisy and frequently disruptive. And they're untidy.'

'So am I. My mother despairs of me.'

The whole thing sounded like a recipe for disaster and Christian slid a finger inside the collar of his shirt. 'I don't need help.'

There was a crash from one of the bedrooms upstairs and Lara flinched and pulled a face. 'No?' She tilted her head back and glanced up at the ceiling as if she was expecting a crack to appear. 'I'll go and see to the repairs while you think about my offer.'

CHAPTER FIVE

Why had she mentioned moving in?

It had been a silly, impulsive suggestion. Wishful thinking on her part, because she couldn't imagine anything more perfect than being a part of his lovely, noisy family for Christmas. And Christian obviously needed some help.

But one look at his face had been enough to tell her that he wasn't ever going to say yes to her suggestion. He was obviously used to being pursued by women and equally used to smoothly fending them off.

The chemistry between them clearly unsettled him and he hadn't seemed convinced by her assurance that she didn't want a relationship any more than he did.

He was obviously fiercely protective of his children.

Had they suffered a great deal?

They seemed fine to her, but she barely knew them so she probably wasn't in a position to judge.

Lara took the stairs two at a time and found herself on a bright, spacious landing. The light poured in from large windows and she paused for a moment as she noticed the removal boxes stacked against the wall.

Her head full of questions, she walked a few paces, her feet echoing on the polished wooden floor. In her mind she was already furnishing the place. A large rug to add warmth to the landing, wooden bookshelves to store all those boxes of books. Tall plants that would flourish in the natural light.

It was a beautiful family home, she thought dreamily as she followed the direction of the noise.

Who would have thought that Christian Blake had a house in the smartest part of Notting Hill? Consultants earned good salaries, of course, but all the same…

Another crash from one of the rooms made her jump and Lara switched off her dreams and hurried towards the sound of sobbing.

Pushing open a door, she found herself in Aggie's bedroom.

'I can't find them anywhere. I've emptied all the boxes and they're gone.' Aggie was sobbing noisily, surrounded by the contents of a toy box. 'I need them for the nativity play.'

Lara scooped her off the floor and sat down on a chair with Aggie in her lap. Her blonde curls smelt of shampoo. 'What do you need for the nativity play?'

'Wings.' Her sobs increased and Lara heard Christian's tread on the stairs.

'Don't cry, Aggie. We'll find the wings.'

'What's happened now?' He stood in the doorway, his eyes on his daughter, his voice incredibly patient. 'Aggie?'

'I'm supposed to be an angel and I forgot to tell you. There's a letter in my schoolbag. I need an angel costume.'

Christian dragged his hands through his hair. 'An angel costume? What exactly does that involve? How long do I have to produce the thing?'

There was a faint note of panic in his voice that made Lara smile. She'd seen him display nerves of steel when he coped with critically injured patients, but faced with the task of providing a child with an angel costume, he looked seriously flustered.

Aggie's lip wobbled. 'I can't remember. Monday. Or maybe Tuesday.'

'She needs it by the last Wednesday of term.' Chloe appeared in the doorway. 'The junior nativity is on the Wednesday. It's another week and a half away.'

'Well, that's fine because we have plenty of time.' Lara smiled. 'I can provide an angel costume. And brand-new wings.'

Aggie sniffed. 'I'm supposed to be a white angel.'

'No problem. They sell them at the store where I'm working. I'll buy you a beautiful pair.' Aware that Christian was looking at her, Lara gently deposited Aggie on the floor and stood up, suddenly wondering whether he was about to object. 'Is it OK with you if I deal with the costume?'

His eyes locked on hers and his voice was rough. 'I don't think that would be a good idea.'

'Dad!' Chloe gave him an astonished look. 'Are you mad? You can't make an angel costume! How can it possibly not be a good idea?'

He let out a long breath. 'Because it isn't that simple.'

'Why not? Dad, someone is offering to help,' Chloe said. 'Say yes and say it fast, before she changes her mind.'

Christian ran a hand over his face, looking like a man with an impossible decision to make. Then he let his hand drop to his side and looked at Lara. 'All right.' He spoke the words reluctantly. 'It would be great if you could help Aggie with a costume. Thank you.'

'Good. That's settled, then.'

Christian stooped and lifted Aggie into his arms. 'Stop crying. Lara's going to make you a costume.'

'And will you come and see me in the play? I've got lines to say.'

'He can't, Aggie. You know he's working. He can't just take time off like that.' Chloe leaned against the doorframe. 'They might let me watch you. Last year we got to watch the little ones.'

'I'm not little!' Aggie wailed. 'I want Dad. And Lara. Everyone's allowed two people watching.'

'I'll see if I can get someone to cover,' Christian promised, and he looked at Lara again. 'That offer you made— is it still open?'

'The wild, crazy one?' She grinned at him. 'Yes, of course. Why? Are you changing your mind?'

'What's wild and crazy?' Chloe looked at him and then looked at Lara. 'And what is Daddy changing his mind about?'

Christian held out his hand to Chloe. 'We're going to manage without a nanny until Christmas is over.'

'But how?' Chloe sidled over to him and took his hand. 'You can't stop working.'

'Lara has agreed to come and stay for a while. We'll adjust our shifts so that one of us can pick you up from school—'

'Stay for a while—you mean *live here*?' Aggie's eyes were huge and Christian nodded.

'She'll pick you up from school if I'm working and she'll be here if I'm late home from work.'

'But what about the holidays?' Chloe looked up at him. 'You both work in the same place, don't you?'

'Yes, but not always at the same time. One of us will be here with you.'

'Really?' Chloe's face brightened. 'That's cool.'

'Amazingly cool,' Aggie breathed, scrambling to her feet and sliding her hand into Lara's. 'It's way beyond awesome.'

Christian blinked. 'Sorry?'

'Way beyond awesome. I heard it on television.'

Lara covered her mouth with her hand to stop the laughter. She still couldn't quite believe that she was going to move in with this wonderful family. It was so much better than spending a lonely Christmas on her own in her flat.

'What about your own family?' Chloe was looking at her. 'Everyone spends Christmas with their family. Won't they miss you?'

'My family have all gone away for Christmas,' Lara explained, trying to sound cheerful. 'My parents are in their cottage in France and my brother moved to Australia six months ago. I only have two days off at Christmas and it isn't enough for me to go anywhere. So I was going to spend Christmas on my own, but now I'm going to spend it with you.'

'Our mummy lives far away, too,' Aggie said. 'She went away with a suitcase.'

Out of the corner of her eye, Lara sensed Christian's sudden tension and she sat back down again and pulled the little girl onto her lap. 'Why don't you tell me what you'd most like to do this Christmas, Aggie.'

She wanted to make sure that they had a fantastic time.

Aggie snuggled closer. 'Play with my toys. And have a big tree.'

'We can play. And we'll find the best tree in the forest.'

'Who will you sleep with?' Aggie looked up at her. 'If I get lonely I sleep in Chloe's bed. She doesn't mind as long as I don't wet it. You could sleep there, too, if you get lonely. Or you could sleep with Daddy. He's got more room in his bed.'

'She can't sleep with Daddy!' Her tone appalled, Chloe glanced towards her father. 'Dad—'

'You're talking too much, young lady,' Christian drawled, but there was laughter in his eyes as he scooped his daughter into his arms and gave her a look that was supposed to subdue her. 'Lara will have her own room.'

Aggie shuddered. 'No one to share with? But that's lonely, Dad.'

'I'd love to have my own room,' Lara assured her hastily, trying not to think about sharing Christian's bed. *Trying not to think about Christian naked.* 'I won't be lonely at all. It's only for sleeping and we can all have such a lot of fun when we're awake. That's what counts.'

'Really? You're going to come and live here? She's the miracle, Daddy,' Aggie breathed. 'Lara is our miracle.'

Three days later Christian was wondering how one person, especially one as delicately built as Lara, could make such an impact on a house.

Her clothes were strewn over chairs, her shoes were left lying in the hall as a deadly trap for the unwary, and the whole house suddenly seemed filled with her enthusiastic, noisy chatter and endless jokes.

In a matter of days his entire house was transformed from an empty, imposing building into a chaotic family home. For the first time since he'd collected the keys from the estate agent, it actually felt as though someone lived there.

And she worked incredibly hard.

The pile of unpacked boxes diminished and books appeared in the previously empty bookcases. Lamps were placed on tables and paintings hung on walls.

But the biggest transformation was the noise level.

For months, the only real noise in the place had been Aggie's chatter, but suddenly the whole place seemed to have come alive. The rooms and the spacious hallway reverberated with ear-splitting shrieks and laughter. Even Chloe was talking more. And then there was the music. Classical, jazz, pop, it didn't seem to matter as long as something was playing day and night.

And Lara sang all the time. She sang when she cooked, she sang in the shower and she sang as she put the children to bed.

She was the sunniest, noisiest, most positive person he'd ever met.

She was also the only woman who hadn't made a pass at him.

But the tension between them was mounting to almost unbearable levels.

He'd given her a room on the top floor of the house, well away from his, but that hadn't stopped her prancing unself-consciously into the kitchen at breakfast-time in a skimpy strap top and a pair of little shorts which she obviously wore to bed.

She seemed totally unaware of her body.

Unfortunately for him, he wasn't similarly immune.

In fact, there were moments when Lara's body seemed to be the only thing he could think about.

Gritting his teeth, Christian tried to concentrate on the blood results that he was holding in his hand.

'You look distracted.' As if to torture him still further, Lara appeared at his side, a smile on her face. 'I just came to tell you that I'm leaving in five minutes. Jane says I can go a bit early so I'll pick up a few things for dinner on my way home.'

Wondering why she had such a volcanic effect on his libido, Christian wrestled against the temptation to power her back against the door. He should kiss her. *Kill or cure.* Except that he knew that in his case that approach wouldn't work. 'You don't have to cook dinner.' As far as he was concerned, the less contact the better.

She could have a sandwich in her room. And lock her door.

'I like cooking. Are those Mrs Neel's blood results?' Apparently oblivious to his struggle for control, she peered over his shoulder at the results. 'Oh, dear, that haemoglobin is very low. Are you referring her?'

'To the gastroenterologists.' He put the results down on the trolley and looked at her. 'Is everything working out all right for you? You seem to be spending your entire free time unpacking boxes at the moment. Perhaps this wasn't such a great idea. Maybe you should just move back to your flat.' *Did he want her to move back to her flat?* He no longer knew the answer to that question.

All he knew was that his body was simmering with frustration.

He was thinking things that he shouldn't be thinking.

'Why would I want to move back to my flat?' Lara gave him a curious look. 'But I do want to ask you about Chloe. She's very quiet, isn't she? She seems a bit…insecure.'

Christian tensed. If there was one thing guaranteed to dampen his libido it was the enormity of his responsibility towards his daughters. 'Both of them are insecure, but they show it in different ways. Chloe is quiet. Aggie is clingy.'

'Yes, I'd noticed that she never lets go of your hand.'

'She's stopped wetting the bed now and she's sleeping again, so that's progress.' He paused for a moment, wondering why on earth he was revealing the intimate details of his family when he never talked about personal matters. 'I think we're doing all right. I worried about moving house but I think it was the right thing to do.'

'Poor things.' Lara's voice was soft. 'It must have been very hard for them. For all of you.'

'Chloe still worries me. She's always been the serious, studious one but she's been even more so since Fiona left.'

'She worries about you.'

'And I worry about her.' He ran a hand over his face. 'She's growing up so fast. Too fast. There are probably all sorts of conversations that I'm supposed to be having with her, but I have no idea how to start any of them.'

Would he have felt more confident if he'd had sons?

'I think you should just relax a bit and do and say what feels right at the time. She's a very sensitive girl. If you're tense, she'll pick it up.'

'How do you know so much about my daughter in such a short time?'

Lara smiled up at him. 'I've been watching the interaction between you. She's very intuitive and old enough to know that you have feelings, too.'

Christian frowned. 'It's *her* feelings I'm worried about. She doesn't understand why her mother left and now she spends her time nurturing the rest of the family.'

Lara nodded. 'She's probably not telling you how she feels because she doesn't want to worry you. She's sort of put herself into the role of mother, hasn't she? What she needs is to see you happy and enjoying your life. I suspect that, when that happens, she'll relax and think about herself a bit more. You should be proud that you have a child who cares about other people so much.'

'It makes her vulnerable. She cares too much.'

'You can't care too much, Christian,' she said softly, 'not within a family. Love is the glue that holds a family together. It's love that turns flaws into endearing traits. Love is the oil that prevents friction.'

Deciding that love wasn't a topic that he wanted to pursue with Lara, Christian swiftly changed the subject. 'I promised Aggie I'd try and be home in time to read her a bedtime story but if I'm not…'

'Then I'll read it,' Lara said cheerfully. 'What would you like for supper? Any special requests?'

She made it sound cosy and intimate, and Christian inhaled sharply. 'I'll make myself something.' He wasn't at all sure that he wanted to put his self-control to the test by spending the evening lingering over a meal with Lara.

Lara tilted her head to one side and studied him. 'Not very good at accepting help, are you, Dr Blake? If you're going to argue with my every suggestion, this whole experience is going to be exhausting.'

Christian was about to answer when Jane hurried up to them 'Thirty-year-old man with chest pains on his way in. Why is everyone having chest pains at the moment?'

'It's the stress of Christmas,' Lara murmured, turning to walk towards the staffroom. 'Peace on earth, chest pains to all men.'

Christian watched her go, his gaze sliding from her shiny blonde hair to the tempting curve of her hips.

Putting his daughters' feelings before his own needs suddenly didn't seem as easy as it had before she'd moved in.

Lara slipped the casserole into the oven next to the baked potatoes.

Aggie appeared at her shoulder. 'I'm hungry.'

'That's because you didn't eat your tea,' Lara said mildly, closing the oven door securely and straightening up. 'It's still on the table if you want to finish it.'

Aggie eyed her plate. 'I'm allergic to broccoli.'

'What happens when you eat broccoli?'

'My stomach sort of heaves.'

Lara hid a smile. 'We'll compromise. Eat half. And finish the nuggets.'

'They tasted funny.'

'They were home-made,' Chloe said as she put down her knife and fork. 'And they were delicious. Much better than the frozen muck the last two nannies have given us. Aggie, sit down and eat your broccoli. Don't be difficult.'

Aggie pouted. 'Mummy never cared if I ate broccoli.'

'That's because she was never here to see what you ate,' Chloe said. 'She was always working. Just eat, Aggie.'

Aggie opened her mouth to argue then closed it again and sat down at the table. 'Just half, then.' She ate quickly, watching Lara all the while. 'That thing in the oven smells nice. Is it for Daddy's tea?'

'If he wants it. I suppose he might eat at the hospital.'

'I hope not because then he'll be late and he promised to read me a story,' Aggie said, but Lara wasn't listening to her. She was watching Chloe.

She'd seen the dark shadows flicker in the depths of her eyes at the mention of Christian eating at the hospital.

He was all they had.

It must be difficult for them when he worked late.

'Was there something in particular you wanted to talk to him about?' she asked gently, and Chloe gave a quick shake of her head.

'No. Nothing. It doesn't matter if he's late. I know he's busy.'

'He has to read my story,' Aggie announced again, and Chloe gave a bright smile as she poured herself some water.

'Of course he'll read your story if he can. You know he always does.'

Lara peeled a couple of satsumas and put them on a

plate in the middle of the table. 'Have you told him you'd like him to be home?'

Chloe dropped her eyes. 'He doesn't have any choice how late he stays at the hospital.'

'The absolute worstest thing is when he works on Saturday,' Aggie said glumly, 'because then I miss my swimming.'

'Oh, I have amazing plans for Saturday,' Lara said cheerfully as she chopped up an apple. 'We're going to make our own Christmas decorations.'

Aggie stared. 'We are?'

'Definitely. But first we're going to sort through the last of those boxes and finish unpacking. When we've done that, we're going to go into the garden and cut some of that beautiful holly and decorate the house. And then we're going to make our own decorations and then on Sunday perhaps we'll buy the tree.'

Aggie carefully balanced her knife and fork over the remains of the broccoli. 'Already? Last year Daddy forgot and we didn't get one until Christmas Eve and there was only one in the shop and it had hardly any needles left.'

He forgot? Was that when his wife had walked out?

Seeing the drawn expression on Chloe's face, Lara assumed that it must have been.

'Well, this year your tree is going to have plenty of needles. If you've finished that, you can eat some fruit.' Deciding to diplomatically ignore the broccoli, Lara cleared Aggie's plate. 'And then you can try on your new angel costume.'

'You've made me an angel costume?'

'Not exactly. I paid a quick trip to the shops,' Lara confessed, reaching for the bag. 'Try it on. Chloe? I picked up some paint cards when I was in the shops. I thought you might like to choose a colour for your bedroom. Have a look at them.'

Chloe stared at her. 'My bedroom?' She shook her head. 'My bedroom is fine. It can wait.'

'I have an idea, but if you hate it, you must tell me.' Lara reached for Aggie's crayons, which were strewn over the table, and started to colour in broad strokes. 'Look at this. How about we paint three wide stripes around two of the walls? Different colours. Purple, orange and blue. Not bright ones. Pastel. Disgusting or amazing?'

Chloe looked at the sketch and then at the paint colours that Lara pushed in front of her. 'A-amazing,' she stammered. 'But that would take ages and be really hard.'

'No. It would just take patience, a sense of humour and lots of masking tape,' Lara said blithely, turning to look at Aggie who had wriggled into the costume. 'Now, that is what I call an angel costume! Do you like it?'

Aggie stared down at herself. 'It's way beyond awesome,' she breathed, and Lara grinned at Chloe.

'Does that mean she likes it?'

Chloe laughed. 'It means she likes it.'

CHAPTER SIX

CHRISTIAN opened the front door and then paused on the threshold, wondering for a moment whether he'd walked into the wrong house.

Lively Christmas music blared through the tall, elegant building, punctuated by the steady thumping of feet and shrieks of female laughter. The thumps and bangs were so loud that he glanced upwards, wondering how many more thumps it would take to bring the ceiling down.

Were they having a party?

Christian gave a faint smile. Whatever Lara was doing with his children, they were clearly enjoying it and that was all he cared about. If necessary, he'd pay someone to fix the ceiling.

He closed the door behind him, shutting out the bitterly cold December evening, and the delicious smell of garlic and herbs wafting from the kitchen made him realise how hungry he was. Suddenly he was glad that he hadn't succeeded in stopping Lara from cooking,

He hung up his coat and then followed the sound of laughter. Pushing open the drawing-room door, he stopped in amazement.

Chloe, Aggie and Lara were all wearing toy antlers and gyrating furiously to a rock and roll song about Rudolph.

Christian watched his children for a moment and then he looked at Lara.

And continued to look.

She was wearing a tartan miniskirt with a black jumper and thick black tights, and she moved her whole body in perfect time to the music, somehow managing to combine both grace and energy as she executed a deceptively simple dance that Chloe and Aggie were both trying to emulate. Her legs went on for ever and her blonde hair and blue eyes provided a splash of colour against the unrelieved black of her jumper. With the brown, furry antlers on her head, she looked young, uninhibited and—*gorgeous*?

Captivated by the sudden injection of life into his home, Christian could have watched her for ever but Aggie noticed him and gave a shriek.

'Daddy's home!' She raced towards him and leapt, forcing Christian to catch her in mid-air. 'We're playing discos. Lara calls it the Rudolph Jive. She says it's great for warming you up on a cold day.'

Lara stopped dancing and pushed strands of blonde hair away from her pink face. Her eyes sparkled with humour as she smiled at him. 'Hi, there! I couldn't find the controls to turn up your central heating. It was dance or freeze. This is a big house. I'm used to living in a tiny flat. If I just turn on the hairdryer, the place heats up so fast I have to open the window.'

'The boiler is in the basement. I'll show you how to adjust it later.' He stroked Aggie's hair and glanced over her shoulder at Chloe. Her cheeks were flushed and her eyes were sparkling with laughter, but there was a wary look in her eyes that hadn't been there when he'd first entered the room.

Was it him? Had he done something?

Did she blame him for the fact that her mother had left?

'Hello, Daddy.' She rushed to turn the music down. 'Did you have a good day?'

Christian frowned, wondering why she felt the need to stop what she was doing. It didn't escape his notice that in comparison with Aggie's unselfconscious exuberance, Chloe was painfully, almost unnaturally well behaved. He studied her for a moment, trying to work out the problem and failing. He wanted her to act like the child she still was and it seemed as though she'd been doing exactly that until he'd walked into the room.

Why had his sudden entrance had that effect on her?

Suddenly he wished that baby daughters were delivered with manuals. He had absolutely no idea how he should be handling this current phase in her life. What if her subdued behaviour had nothing to do with the divorce? What if she was being bullied at school? *What if there was a boy?*

He broke out in a cold sweat and then reassured himself that there was no way that Chloe had boy trouble. *Yet.* But boy trouble would undoubtedly come in time, and he would be expected to help her with her problems.

Lara was still trying to catch her breath. She didn't appear to notice anything amiss so he just smiled at Chloe. 'I had a good day, thanks, sweetheart. How about you?'

'Very good. Lara's a great cook. We made nuggets together and she's made you casserole.'

Aggie bounced in his arms. 'And she's going to decorate the whole house and Chloe's bedroom, and, if I help unpack the last of the boxes, can we go and get a huge tree on Sunday?'

Christian's eyes slid to Lara. Her cheeks were still pink from the dancing, her blonde hair kicked up at the edges and her full mouth was curved in a wide, happy smile.

'Sorry. Hope I haven't overstepped the mark,' she said breathlessly, waving a hand in front of her face in an attempt to cool herself down. 'You're working on Saturday so I thought the girls and I could spend the day transforming the house into something Christmassy. But if you'd rather we didn't…'

'That sounds like an excellent idea. I have a decorator that I used when we first moved in. I'll call him. The whole house used to be red.'

'I loved it,' Aggie sighed. 'It was like living inside a fire engine.'

'How relaxing.' Lara laughed, exchanging a look of sympathy with Christian. 'If your decorator is free, that would be great. He could do Chloe's room and that would leave us free to concentrate on the rest of the house.'

'Lara made you dinner.' Aggie jiggled in his arms. 'Will you read to me now or do you have to go and eat?'

His eyes slid to Lara in a silent question but she shrugged, completely relaxed.

'Dinner can wait. It's just a casserole. I didn't want to make anything elaborate because I didn't know what time you'd be in or whether you would have eaten. Read to Aggie. It's much more important. You can eat when she's asleep. Chloe—why don't you and I finish that design for your bedroom?'

Christian tried not to remember the number of times that his wife had lost her temper when he'd wanted to relax with the children after a day at work.

But Lara wasn't his wife, he reminded himself. 'Have you eaten?'

'Not yet.' She pulled the antlers from her head and dropped them onto the sofa. 'I'll grab some casserole later. Or make some toast. Whatever.'

'We'll put the girls to bed and then eat together.' Like
one big happy family. He almost laughed as he listened to
himself, wondering with cynical amusement which of his
suggestions sounded more intimate. Eating together or
putting his children to bed? He lowered Aggie to the floor,
wondering why on earth he'd agreed to Lara's offer to
move in with them. 'Go and get into your pyjamas, clean
your teeth and I'll come and read to you.'

And then he was going to pour himself a large drink and
try not to think about Lara's legs.

Lara emptied the bath, cleared up the toys, checked on
Chloe, who was reading a book on her bed, and then returned to the kitchen.

She lifted the large casserole dish out of the oven and
placed it in the middle of the table, then added warmed
plates, baked potatoes and a bowl of broccoli.

She'd considered serving dinner in the formal dining
room and had then thought better of it. It didn't take a genius
to know that Christian wasn't entirely comfortable with the
situation so it would be more sensible to eat in the kitchen.
It would look less as though she was trying to be romantic.

She was humming to herself and removing a bottle of
mineral water from the fridge when Christian strolled
into the room.

'You're always singing.'

'Sorry. I like singing.'

His eyes slid to the bottle of water. 'Given that neither of
us are working this evening, I think we can do better than that.'

It was so much easier to resist him when he was dressed
in a blue scrub suit, Lara thought desperately, flattening
herself against the fridge door as he crossed the room
towards her.

He'd showered and changed into jeans and a chunky roll-neck jumper. His hair was still slightly damp but he hadn't bothered to shave and his jaw was dark with stubble. He looked impossibly sexy and for a distinctly unsettling moment she felt her stomach roll over, as if she were on an extreme ride at a theme park.

She contemplated crawling inside the fridge in order to cool herself down but opted instead for clutching the chilled water against her chest.

Apparently oblivious to the emotions that were threatening to overwhelm her, he reached past her and pulled out a bottle of wine. His arm brushed against hers and the contact was like an electric shock. Lara gritted her teeth and closed her eyes briefly. When she opened them it was to find him looking at her, and the fire blazing from his blue eyes made her realise that she wasn't the only one who was struggling with the situation.

She waited for him to speak but he said nothing. He just looked at her and awareness exploded between them.

'Is it me or is it getting hot in here?' She gave a weak smile. 'We'd better move before we defrost the fridge. Let's open that wine and drink it.'

His jaw tightened and he moved away and reached for a bottle-opener. 'This thing between us…' he stabbed the cork viciously '…isn't going to go anywhere, Lara.'

So he wasn't denying that the chemistry existed. She made a noise that was something between a whimper and a laugh. 'That's fine by me. I'm off to Australia in a month and a broken heart isn't on my Christmas list.'

He yanked the cork out of the bottle with more force than was necessary and turned to face her, his expression serious. 'So that's settled, then.'

'Yes.' Her eyes met his and they stared at each other for

a long moment. Ignoring her shaking legs, she walked over to the table. 'It would make the process easier if I could find a major flaw in you. Usually I manage it without any help but with you—I don't know, I seem to be struggling.'

'I'd be happy to help.' He lifted two glasses out of the cupboard, the tension visible in his shoulders. 'What sort of flaw are you looking for?'

'Anything, as long as it's big and seriously offputting. OK, let's try something. Here's a question for you. If I handed you a large bar of chocolate, would you eat some of it or all of it?'

'It depends on how hungry I was.'

'Perfect answer!' She felt a rush of relief and sat down on the nearest chair. 'You've just revealed a *major* flaw because I'd eat the whole thing even if I was completely full to bursting. Restraint when it comes to chocolate is a major flaw as far as I'm concerned. You're sunk. We'd never be happy together.'

He put the glasses and the wine down on the table. 'Do you always look for flaws in men?'

'Not intentionally. They just sort of jump out at me. According to my mother, I'm just too fussy, but I don't see how you can be too fussy, do you? I mean, there's no point in spending the rest of your life with a man who makes you shudder, is there?'

Christian gave a faint smile as he poured the wine. 'I think you're right to be fussy. It's easy to make a mistake.' He handed her a glass. 'And then other people suffer.'

Was that what had happened to him? *Had he made a mistake?* 'I don't think your girls are suffering. I think you're a fantastic father and they're jolly lucky to have you,' she said softly. 'And now let's eat. I can't have a conversation as deep as this on an empty stomach and the casserole is getting cold.'

Without giving him the chance to answer, she spooned casserole onto his plate, trying to slow the thud of her heart.

When she'd suggested moving in, it hadn't occurred to her for a moment that she'd find it as difficult as this. She never found men irresistible. Never.

It was just because he was keeping his distance, she thought dryly as she put a baked potato on her plate. If he'd shown anything less than iron self-control, she would have been the one backing off.

He watched her for a long moment. 'Do you always say exactly what's on your mind?'

'Almost always. It's my biggest failing. I find it impossible to think one thing and say another.' She shrugged. 'My mother thinks I'll never find a man until I learn not to talk so much. Which basically means that I'm doomed.'

'You're obviously close to your family.'

'Very.' She put a knob of butter on her baked potato and watched while it melted. 'We grew up on a farm in a pretty corner of Dorset where everyone knew everyone. London has been quite a culture shock for me. Everyone lives parallel lives. No one notices or cares what anyone else is doing.' *And she'd never quite got used to being so far from her family.*

'How long have you worked here?'

'Two years.' Lara added some broccoli to her plate. 'I moved because I wanted the experience of working in the emergency department of a big London teaching hospital. There aren't that many shootings and stabbings in my part of Dorset and our idea of an RTA is a tractor colliding with a hedge. What about you? Why did you move hospitals?'

'The post was too attractive to turn down. The facilities are amazing and there was an opportunity to do research alongside my clinical responsibilities.'

'In other words, extra work.'

'Something like that. And I thought the change might be good. This casserole is great.'

Lara speared a piece of meat with her fork and studied it. 'I probably should have warned you that generally I'm not very domesticated. I'm very untidy and I'm blind to the presence of dirt or dust, but I like my food, so I made sure that I learned to cook. My mother is a wizard in the kitchen.'

'You mentioned that your parents are in France.'

'Yes, they have a house in the Dordogne and they've been spending more and more time there. I suppose they thought that with Tom in Australia and me in London, they may as well go to France over Christmas.' She pushed away the faint feeling of sadness. 'What about your family? Will they join you over Christmas?'

'No.'

She waited for him to say more, but he carried on eating. 'That's it?' She raised her eyebrows. 'That's all you're going to tell me about your family?'

'There's not much to tell. I'm an only child. My parents and I aren't close.' He lifted his wineglass and drank.

'They're not interested in their grandchildren?' She thought about it for a moment. 'My mother drives Tom and me nuts with her constant nagging about our reluctance to provide her with grandchildren to spoil. Your parents aren't the same?'

'Hardly.' His tone was neutral. 'Children, generally, aren't their favourite thing.'

'They had you.'

'Yes, although, I sometimes wonder why. I went to boarding school at seven. Don't look so shocked. It happens.'

'I'm just trying to imagine being sent to boarding

school at the age of seven. Who hugged you when you had a bad day?'

He topped up their glasses. 'No one hugged me. I didn't need anyone to hug me.'

'Everyone needs affection.' Lara put her fork down and reached for her wine. 'So presumably that's why you're so careful about the children's feelings. You've been hurt yourself by the breakdown of an adult relationship.'

He stilled. 'I've never analysed it before.'

'Men never do. Analysis and guilt is a girl thing.' She lifted her glass. 'It's not enough for us to be screwed up— we have to know the *reason* that we're screwed up.'

Her comment raised a smile but then he glanced at her, his gaze curiously intent. 'It's true that I always envisaged having a traditional family one day,' he said softly. 'But that's an out-of-date concept now, isn't it?'

'I don't think so.'

'Then you're unusual.' His smile faded and there was a hard edge to his voice that warned her that they were straying onto sensitive territory.

Perhaps talking about the children would reduce the tension in the atmosphere. 'Did you look in on Chloe?'

'Yes, she was still reading.' Christian toyed with his wineglass. 'It was good to see her dancing and laughing earlier. She seemed more like her old self. Until I turned up.'

'What do you mean, until you turned up?'

'You didn't notice?'

'She seemed fine to me. It probably wasn't a great idea to wind them up before bedtime but I wanted them to get into the Christmas spirit before the weekend.' Lara dropped her eyes to her plate, because the alternative was staring at him. 'Do you think you'd be able to take them to buy a Christmas tree on Sunday? They'd love it if you could.'

'I'll buy one on my way home from work.'

Appalled, she lifted her gaze. 'Where's the fun in that?! They have to help you choose one.'

'They'll argue.'

'Precisely.' Lara put down her knife and fork. 'Very healthy.'

'You're obviously an expert on Christmas.'

'I love Christmas. Don't you?'

His fingers tightened on the stem of his glass. 'No,' he said flatly. 'I don't. Christmas is for families.'

'You're a family, Christian.'

His eyes met hers. 'Rather a fractured family, don't you think?'

'Families aren't all about a mother, father, two children and a dog.' Lara said mildly.

Christian lounged back in his seat. 'Call me old-fashioned, but I still think that's the ideal set-up.'

'Yes.' She stared at him for a moment. 'I suppose I do, too. But life doesn't always turn out the way you plan, does it? And I suppose it's hardly surprising. How anyone ever finds someone that they're compatible with in our busy, hectic world, I don't know. It's like looking for a needle in a haystack.'

'So is that why you booked your ticket to Australia?'

She smiled. 'If you're asking whether Australia is my haystack then the answer is no. I'm just going to see Tom and maybe travel a bit. I'm not looking for a man. I'm sure they're just as flawed in Australia as they are over here. But I need a change. I've worked in various emergency departments for the past four years and I need something more.'

'You'll be missed.' He glanced around the kitchen. 'I haven't thanked you properly for everything you've done with the house. You may not think you're domesticated but you've succeeded in turning an empty house into a home. Things are improving. Chloe's still quiet and I haven't got to the bottom of it but I'm still trying.'

'Perhaps she's just missing her mum.'

'Perhaps. Although, to be honest, Fiona wasn't around much. She was always working.'

Lara recalled Chloe saying something similar. 'It must have been so hard for the children.'

'It happens. Relationships break down every day.' His gaze was faintly mocking. 'I'm not easy to live with.'

Her stomach rolled over and she gave a smile to cover up just how seriously he affected her. 'So now we're back to the flaws again. Go on. Tell me the worst.' She used laughter to conceal her discomfort. 'Do you lose your temper and yell? Or are you untidy? Do you drop your clothes onto the floor when you take them off, instead of putting them away?'

'And, if I do?'

'Then we both know that you'll probably be dropping them on top of mine,' Lara said, her mind again dominated by a disturbing vision of Christian naked. Flustered by her thoughts, she rose to her feet and picked up the rest of the casserole. 'I'll freeze this for another day when neither of us can be bothered to cook.' She lifted the casserole across the work surface and left the lid off so that it would cool.

Christian stood up. 'I think we need to agree on a few house rules.' He cleared the plates and started loading them into the dishwasher. 'The casserole was delicious but I don't expect you to cook for me. It's enough that you're prepared to move in here and help with my daughters. I can look after myself.'

She wished he wasn't standing quite so close. It was impossibly distracting. 'I like cooking and I don't have anyone to cook for anymore.' She sneaked a look at him. 'I'll cook if I'm not working late, but if you're too late home to eat it, it doesn't matter. How's that for a compromise?'

The kitchen door opened and Chloe put her head round. 'I'm going to bed. Good night.'

Christian turned. 'Good night, sweetheart.' His voice was slightly husky. 'Do you want me to come and tuck you in?'

'No need.' Chloe gave a quick smile and shook her head. 'I'll read for a bit and then put my light out. See you in the morning.'

Go after her, Lara urged silently, but Christian stood still, staring at the closed door with a frown on his handsome face.

He stirred. 'I usually tuck her in. Is twelve too old to be kissed good-night? I honestly have no idea.'

Lara tilted her head to one side thoughtfully. 'Well, I've never had children but I wouldn't think that you're ever too old for a hug. I'm still happy to be kissed good-night by the right guy, and I'm twenty-five.'

His jaw tightened. 'Lara—'

'OK, OK, I probably shouldn't have said that.' She lifted a hand and gave a helpless shrug. 'I would have thought she'd appreciate a hug. Probably not at the school gates but in the privacy of your own home…I don't know, Christian. Perhaps you should just not give her the choice and go on up.'

'I sensed that she didn't want me to.'

Lara stood, not knowing what to say. She'd sensed the same thing, but what little girl wouldn't want her dad? Why would Chloe push him away? 'It's almost as if she's afraid she's being a bother.'

'A bother?' Christian turned to look at her, a frown in

his eyes as he considered what she'd said. 'Why would she think that?'

'I honestly don't know. Is it to do with her mother? How does she feel about all that?'

There was a long silence and a muscle flickered in his jaw. 'I have no idea. She refuses to talk about it.'

'She's *never* talked about it?'

'Not really. I've tried, of course, but she always changes the subject really quickly.' Christian glanced towards the closed door. 'She seems more interested in checking that I'm happy. I think I'm probably asking all the wrong questions. I'm just not good at talking to twelve-year-old girls.'

'It can't be an easy thing to talk about.' Lara hesitated. 'Could she be hoping that her mum might come back?'

'No.' His tone was hard. 'I was honest with them on that score. Perhaps too honest, but I didn't want to create hope where there was none.'

Lara thought of her own family and how close they were and didn't bother trying to hide her shock. 'Well, the whole thing must have been pretty traumatic for someone of Chloe's age. It's very unusual for a woman to leave her children. Does she visit them?'

'She's in Hong Kong, so visiting isn't easy. She dropped in once when she had a stopover at Heathrow but she hasn't spent much time in the UK since she left last Christmas. She's an accountant and she was transferred to the Hong Kong office. Very prestigious job.'

Lara looked at him. 'I don't know what to say,' she murmured. 'You must have been devastated.'

He was silent for such a long time that she thought he wasn't going to respond to her statement but then he lifted his head and looked at her. 'I was devastated for the girls.'

She frowned. *What was that supposed to mean?* That he hadn't loved his wife?

'Christian—'

'Move on, Lara,' he said softly. 'My ex-wife isn't my favourite topic of conversation. Perhaps you're right. Perhaps I will go and tuck Chloe in.'

'Perhaps she might chat to me if we're decorating at the weekend.' Lara smiled. 'There's nothing quite so effective as the boredom of painting a room to induce an intimate conversation.'

CHAPTER SEVEN

THE rest of the week was a whirl of work and unpacking.

When she was at home, Lara finished emptying boxes and found homes for all the children's possessions, and, when she was at work, she tried to concentrate on patients and not think about being attracted to Christian.

But it was hard.

Especially once Jane discovered her new living arrangements. 'Christian mentioned that you've moved in to help him with the kids.'

Lara frowned. 'He told you that?'

'Yes. We were chatting.'

'Christian doesn't chat.'

'He does if you force the issue. I don't know which piece of information shocked me most. The fact that he's divorced or the news that you've moved in with him. Why didn't you tell me?!'

'Because I was worried that you might ring my mother.' Lara glanced towards the ambulance bay, waiting for the arrival of an overdose patient. 'She'd jump to the wrong conclusions.'

'You're not involved, then?'

'No.' Lara checked her watch. Ambulance Control had

said five minutes but there was no sign of the patient. 'My love life is as depressingly stagnant as ever.'

'Well, that might change now you're actually living in the same house. You might bump into him naked in the bathroom.' Jane gave her a wicked smile. 'Do me a favour and carry a camera with you, just in case.'

'You're perverted.' Lara stared out of the window. 'And it's a big house. I could walk around naked for a week and not bump into him and, anyway, neither of us is interested in a relationship.'

Jane looked at her. 'I wasn't really talking about a relationship. I was thinking more of passionate sex with a guy who looks like a Greek god. It seems like too perfect an opportunity to waste.'

'Well, I'm going to waste it. He has two children and I'm going to Australia next month.'

'Which gives you plenty of time to have a steamy, no-strings affair. Sounds just about perfect to me. You need some light relief. You work much too hard.' Jane stared thoughtfully through the window. 'Where are they? Do you think the ambulance has crashed?'

'I hope not because we've only just restocked Resus after the last black ice disaster. It's freezing out there.'

'Snow is forecast at the weekend. Can you imagine that?'

'Brilliant. It will make everything really Christmassy.' Lara's mood lifted and Jane gave an irritated frown.

'Do you have to be so relentlessly positive? It's really exhausting for the rest of us. Could you occasionally try and look on the black side, like normal people?'

'I don't see a black side to snow.'

'Of course there's a black side,' Jane said gloomily. 'A mere sprinkling of white dust and the whole city grinds to a halt. Cars slither, people slither, bones are broken...'

'Well, we're stuck here, anyway, so we may as well have some customers.' Lara heard the siren and gave a nod. 'Here we go. Lights, camera, action.'

The paramedics took the unconscious man straight through to Resus and seconds later Christian joined them.

Jack, the paramedic, helped transfer the patient from their stretcher to the resus trolley. 'His name is Gordon Baxter. He's fifty-five, lives with his wife. She went out shopping this morning and found him when she returned. Apparently there was a note telling her not to call the ambulance.'

The team listened to the handover as they worked.

Without delay, Christian intubated the patient and Lara helped Penny insert a line into the patient's vein.

Jack moved the stretcher away and retrieved his blanket. 'He's been treated by the doctor for depression but there were no empty bottles lying around. We looked.'

'Is his wife here?'

'Just giving his details to Fran in Reception.' Jack looked at the man on the trolley. 'Apparently he lost his job six months ago and he's been depressed ever since.'

'Poor man,' Lara murmured, monitoring his pulse rate. 'It's a hundred and forty, Christian.'

His mouth tightened. 'He's taken something. We just need to work out what. Can someone go and question his wife in more detail? Were any of his tablets missing?'

'I'll talk to her,' Jane said immediately, and Lara reached for the ECG machine.

'Let's do a trace.'

'Yes.' Christian was examining the patient, checking his eyes. 'He has a divergent squint and his pupils are unreactive. Penny—we need to check his blood gases.'

Lara attached the ECG leads to the patient and Penny stared at the machine. 'He's in VT.'

'No.' Christian studied the trace. 'It's sinus tachycardia with prolonged conduction. Look…' He drew a finger along the trace. 'The P wave is superimposed on the T wave. That's why it looks like VT.'

Lara stared at the ECG and wondered if she would have spotted the same thing. Maybe. 'Tricyclic antidepressants?'

'Possibly.' Christian nodded. 'Very possibly. Can someone ring his GP's surgery and find out what he was taking, just to be sure?'

Penny looked at them both. 'How do you know it's tricyclics? It could be anything.'

'Not anything,' Christian said calmly as he tested the man's reflexes. 'The signs are there if you know what you're looking for. Lara, you should train as a doctor.'

'I wouldn't know what to do with the salary,' Lara said cheerfully. 'I've been living on nothing for so long.'

At that moment Jane hurried back into the room. 'He's been taking amitryptoline. His wife couldn't find the bottle when she looked in the cupboard so it could be that.'

'We can safely assume that it's amitryptoline. Lara, did you send those bloods off?'

'Yes.' She looked up at him. 'Do you want to give him activated charcoal?'

Christian shook his head. 'Only if it's within an hour of overdose and we're way past that. Jane, do you know if the formulation he was taking was sustained release?'

'It wasn't. I asked.'

'Good.' Christian gave a nod of approval. 'So let's give him 8.4 per cent of sodium bicarbonate. Hopefully, by correcting the hypoxia and acidosis, we'll treat the arrhythmias.'

Lara reached for the ampoule. 'One hundred mils?'

'We'll start with that. Sometimes it produces a dramatic improvement.'

Penny stepped closer. 'Why?'

'It alters protein binding and lowers the amount of active free tricyclic drug.' Christian injected the sodium bicarbonate and looked up. 'How's his blood pressure?'

'Dropping,' Lara murmured, her eyes on the screen.

'Can we elevate the foot of the trolley? And let's give 1 milligram of glucagon. Jane, can you ring the physicians? He's going to need to be admitted.'

They worked to stabilise the patient and then the physicians arrived.

Christian went with Jane to talk to the man's wife and Lara helped transfer the patient to the ward.

When she returned to Resus, Christian was in the room, finishing the notes.

'Will he live, do you think?' Lara felt a rush of sadness as she thought about the man lying still and unresponsive on the trolley. 'I hate to think of anyone feeling that desperate. It must be awful for his wife.'

'She's blaming herself. It's the usual question of "what if?" What if she'd come home earlier from shopping? What if she'd decided to go on another day? It's hard for her.' Christian finished writing and walked across the room to the sink. 'Let's hope he'll be OK.'

'Christmas can be a difficult time of year.'

'Yes.' His answer was surprisingly terse and she studied his profile, remembering what he'd said about his wife leaving at Christmas.

'Did she leave before or after?'

He took a long time washing his hands and, for a moment, she wondered if he'd even heard her question. Then he turned off the water, dried his hands and turned to look at her. 'After. Just.' He gave a short laugh that was markedly lacking in humour. 'I think she imagined that the children might be so pleased with their presents that they wouldn't notice that she wasn't around.'

Lara couldn't bear to think about how awful it must have been. 'They must have been very shocked.'

'To begin with, Aggie didn't really see a difference because her mother was always jetting off to different parts of the world so her absence wasn't a rarity. It took a while for it to sink in. But Chloe…' He broke off and his mouth tightened. 'Chloe was devastated. For weeks she seemed to shrink into herself and then she just quietly got on with her life.'

'And you?'

'I applied for this job and we moved house.'

'Based on the principle that three major life changes are better than one?' She pulled a face. 'You certainly believe in piling on the stress, Dr Blake.'

'I thought moving house might be good for all of us. And the house is nearer to the girls' school.'

'And was moving a good thing?'

He dried his hands. 'I think so. Apart from the fact that Chloe is far too quiet, they seem more stable.'

'And what about you? How are you?'

'It isn't about me.' He frowned, as though he considered the question strange. 'It's about the children. They didn't choose to be in this situation.'

'And you did?'

Something bleak flickered in his eyes. 'No. But I should have foreseen it. We were a disaster waiting to happen. My wife wasn't good at relationships. And apparently I'm not an easy man to be married to. That's got to be a flaw. You might want to remember that one, Lara.'

She sighed. 'Sorry, but that would only count as a flaw if I was planning to marry you. Given that my longest relationship is three dates, I think that's an unlikely scenario.

I need a flaw that will kill the chemistry stone dead. I thought your chocolate restraint was bad, but apparently it isn't bad enough.'

They looked at each other for a long moment and Lara felt her mouth dry and her heart bump hard against her chest.

It didn't matter what they said or did, the chemistry was there, sizzling away like a high-voltage power cable.

She wanted to kiss him. Just once. To satisfy her curiosity.

And perhaps he read her thoughts because he drew breath sharply and a muscle flickered in his hard jaw. 'Lara—there are some instincts and urges that should be ignored. This is one of them.'

Her whole body burning with frustration, she ran her tongue over her lips to try and moisten them. 'Right. I'm sure that's absolutely the right decision.'

His eyes dropped to her mouth, lingered there for a moment and then he turned sharply and strode out of Resus, shouldering the door open so violently that it crashed against the wall.

Lara flinched and stared after him in helpless frustration.

The chemistry between them was virtually setting fire to the building and he was walking away from it?

She wanted to ask him for a few hints and tips because she wasn't finding it anywhere near as easy to handle as he clearly was.

Then she looked at the door, which was still swinging from the force of his exit.

Maybe he wasn't finding it that easy, either.

Deciding that what she needed was to throw herself into her work and stop dreaming about kissing Christian, she walked back round to the main area of the emergency department to start working her way through the steady stream of patients that poured through the doors on a daily basis. All required concentration and focus. But none prevented her from thinking about kissing Christian.

By the end of her shift, she was becoming impatient with herself.

This was completely ridiculous.

She'd never felt this way about a man and she didn't understand why she was feeling this way now.

It had to be because a relationship just wasn't possible.

Because she couldn't have it, she wanted it.

Determined to think about something other than Christian, she wandered through to Reception to talk to Fran, hoping for distraction.

She found her standing on a chair, pinning metres of tinsel around the reception area.

Lara handed her another rope of tinsel. 'You look unreasonably cheerful for a woman fighting at the front line.'

'I *am* cheerful. I met a man last night.' Fran hugged a piece of tinsel to her chest and beamed. 'Oh, Lara, he was *gorgeous*.'

Lara thought about the psychic's prediction. 'Did you use contraception?'

'Lara!! I can't believe you just asked me that!' Fran covered her mouth and started to laugh, and Lara gave a sheepish smile.

'Sorry.' She stooped and picked up a pile of mistletoe that was lying on the floor. 'So tell me all about him.'

'He's a fireman. I met him when he brought that little boy in a couple of weeks ago.'

'The one who had his leg stuck in the bicycle wheel? Oh, yes, I remember him. Are you seeing him again?'

'Tonight.'

'Good. Well, I hope you have— Make sure you don't—' Deciding that there was no best way to tell someone that a psychic had predicted she'd be pregnant by Christmas, Lara waved the mistletoe. *It was all nonsense, anyway.* 'Where are you planning to put this? Not in Reception, surely? It's asking for trouble. Somebody is bound to eat the berries and sue us.'

'It's going in the staffroom.' Fran jumped down from the chair. 'I thought it might liven up everyone's working day.'

Lara looked at the mistletoe in her hand.

Why not?

It might be the only cure for her problem. It had always worked before. 'Good idea.' She gave Fran a casual smile. 'I'll go and pin it somewhere obvious.'

Lara strolled back down the corridor but instead of turning left to the staffroom, she turned right towards Christian's office. His door was open and he was on the phone, but the moment he saw her his brows rose questioningly. He swiftly terminated the phone call and rose to his feet. 'Problems?'

'I'm afraid so.' She closed the door behind her and gave an apologetic smile. 'Bit of an emergency going on here. I need your help with something.'

Restoring her sanity.

He glanced at the clock on the wall. 'Aren't you supposed to be going home?'

'I'm going home right after this,' she assured him, her heart pounding as she watched him walk around his desk towards her, concern in his eyes. 'I just need you to do something for me.'

'What's that?'

He was so close to her now that she could hardly breathe. Feeling reckless and daring, she rose on tiptoe and the mistletoe slipped from her fingers as she slid her arms round his neck and touched her mouth to his.

His shock was palpable.

Her fingertips registered the sudden tension in his broad shoulders, the hesitation. He stood rigid, his hands by his sides. For a moment she thought he was going to step back and break the connection. But then he brought his hands up and slid them up her back, hauled her against him and took over the kiss.

His mouth was hot and demanding and he powered her back against the door of his office, his body hard against hers as he finally submitted to the violent attraction that they'd both been fighting for weeks. Or had it been months?

She no longer had any sense of time.

His hands slid into her hair and his mouth plundered hers, the astonishing skill of his kiss driving the breath from her body and all coherent thought from her brain.

Somewhere deep inside her she registered that this wasn't turning out quite the way she'd planned, but she felt too dizzy to work out exactly where her plan had taken a wrong turn.

It was the most exciting, erotic moment of her life and, if she'd been able to think, she would have realised that she was out of control for the first time ever. And the kiss wasn't enough. She wanted to touch him. She had to touch him.

Dropping her hands from his neck, she slid them under the top of his scrub suit, feeling hard, male muscle and the tantalising brush of body hair against the tips of her seeking fingers.

'You feel so good,' she gasped against his mouth, sliding her hand around his back. 'Kiss me again. You have to kiss me again.'

'I'm kissing you.' His voice rough, he growled the words against her lips, one of his hands still locked in her hair, while the other slid under her clothing. His touch maddeningly seductive, he stroked his hand down her spine and then pulled her pelvis against his in a gesture as erotic as it was possessive.

She felt him, hard and ready through the fabric of his scrub suit, and reality suddenly sliced through her muddled thoughts.

What was she doing?

What had started as a light-hearted kiss had become deadly serious and she knew that one of them had to stop.

And judging from the purposeful slide of Christian's hand against her quivering flesh, it wasn't going to be him.

'Christian—' Dragging her mouth from his with a supreme effort, she put a hand in the centre of his chest to try and create some distance. Without distance there was no hope for them. 'We have to stop. We can't do this here.'

Ignoring her muttered protest, he cupped her face in his hands, brought her face back to his and started to kiss her again. She tumbled head first back into paradise, light exploding in her head and her nerve endings shrieking with an almost unbearable excitement.

For a moment she allowed herself to be swept along and then she dragged her mouth from his and shook her head. 'No.'

The word must have registered because he stilled, his mouth a breath away from hers. 'No?'

'No.' It took all her willpower to say the word, especially when she saw the simmering passion in his eyes.

'Lara—you started this.' His lips brushed hers with seductive purpose and she gave a low whimper and swayed towards him.

'I didn't.'

'You did.' He slid his hands slowly down her arms. 'You grabbed me.'

'I just gave you a quick kiss. You were the one who turned it into a—a—'

'A what?'

A feast? *A rampant seduction?* 'A passionate clinch.'

'You kissed me, Lara. What did you expect me to do?' He released her and took a step back, his attention caught by something on the floor. 'What the hell is that?' He stared at the squashed mess on the floor and she gave a strangled laugh.

'I think it's what's left of the mistletoe. You must have trampled on it.'

'Why is there mistletoe on my floor?'

'I must have dropped it when you kissed me.'

'Let's get this straight.' His eyes burned into hers. '*You* kissed *me.*'

'Yes, all right. I kissed you. I don't think it really matters who started it. But I think the mistletoe is beyond help. Oh, dear. I was planning to kiss you *under* the mistletoe, not on top of it.' She looked at the remains of the mistletoe. 'That's not good. Fran's going to kill me. That bunch of berries had sole responsibility for departmental excitement this Christmas. I'm not sure that mistletoe purée has the same effect on people's libido.' Her attempt at humour did nothing to defuse the tension in the atmosphere and his eyes drifted back to her mouth.

'There's masses of mistletoe growing on the apple trees in my garden. Help yourself.'

She didn't want to feel this way. 'Having just seen what a small bunch can do,' she croaked, 'I don't think we'd better risk it, do you?'

His gaze lifted to hers. 'So what was the problem? When you came into my office you said there was a problem.'

'The chemistry between us is proving to be a bit of a

problem,' she whispered. 'I thought kissing you would solve everything. It's the quickest way I know to expose a flaw.'

'So now what happens, Lara? Perhaps I'm being a little slow, but so far I haven't spotted a flaw.' His voice was soft and she gave a whimper of frustration and backed away.

'I don't know what happens now. It wasn't supposed to be like this. It's all your fault!'

'*My* fault?' He raised an eyebrow. 'You're the one that came in here, carrying mistletoe.'

'Yes.' She glared at him. 'But you did it all wrong! The kiss, I mean.'

'What was wrong with it?'

'Nothing. That's what I mean. It was perfect. *And it wasn't supposed to be*. It was supposed to be revolting or at the very least boring.'

He studied her carefully. 'You've obviously had a wonderful experience of kissing.'

'Well, usually there's something wrong.' She licked her lips and tried to concentrate. 'You know, too wet and dribbly, seriously fumbly, garlic breath—the list is endless.'

'I think I'm finally starting to understand why your record is three dates.' He turned away from her and walked back to his desk. 'I suggest we both forget that this happened. And don't bring plants with berries into my office again.'

She stared at his back. Her whole body was humming with awareness. 'But what do we do now? The kiss didn't work.'

'We forget it.'

'Right. We forget it.' Her voice croaked as she repeated his words. 'You think that's the best approach? You don't think we could just—'

'No.' His voice was terse and his shoulders rigid. 'We couldn't.'

His self-discipline was admirable, she thought miserably. 'Right. So we're going to forget it. I'll just go and write that out a hundred times just in case I forget that I'm supposed to forget.'

Lara tried to forget. She tried really, really hard.

Over the next few days, she threw herself into work but she found it impossible to wipe Christian from her thoughts.

It was as if that one kiss had awakened her body and suddenly it refused to behave. She thought about him. She dreamt about him.

And to make the situation all the more frustrating, it was obvious that he wasn't suffering the same degree of emotional and physical torment.

Both at work and at home, he was cool and detached and clearly had no problem whatsoever in forgetting the kiss they'd shared.

They worked shoulder to shoulder in Resus but his gaze didn't linger and he only spoke when it related to patient care.

At home he spent time with his daughters and she spent more time in her room.

But nothing stopped her thinking about him. And wanting. And that was infuriating.

She wasn't supposed to meet someone who interested her just weeks before she left the country.

And she wasn't supposed to fall for a man who clearly didn't want a relationship.

In desperate need of someone to make her see sense, she rooted out Jane in the staffroom. 'I need some help. I have a serious problem.'

'You've killed a patient?'

Lara glared at her. 'I mean it—I need help. I'm in trouble.'

'Oh, dear.' Jane dropped a syringe into the sharps bin. 'The psychic was right all along and you're pregnant with quads?'

'Jane!'

'Sorry.' Her friend peered at her. 'You look terrible. What's wrong?'

'Christian is what's wrong. I've really fallen for him.'

Jane grinned. 'So you're human after all.'

'This isn't funny. I need to find some flaws in him and I need to find them urgently.'

'Why do you want flaws? Turns out he isn't married after all. So go for it.'

'He doesn't want to go for it and neither do I! I *can't* go for it! I have plans and they don't involve getting mixed up with a man who doesn't want a relationship. And I don't want a relationship either! In a few weeks' time I'm off to Australia for an indefinite period.' Lara paced the room, her lower lip caught between her teeth. 'Why does life have to be so complicated? For twenty-five years I meet men who make me cringe and then finally when I'm about to go off on the trip of a lifetime I meet a man who is bloody perfect!'

Jane lifted her eyebrows. 'I've never heard you swear before!'

'Well, *I'm swearing now!*' Lara covered her face with her hands and shook her head. 'Oh, this is *such* a mess! What am I going to do?'

'Have sex with him?'

'Oh, please! He has two little girls! The only time when they're not around, we're in Resus. When would we have sex? Where? And anyway, that wouldn't solve anything. It isn't an option.' *He wasn't interested.* Lara let her hands drop to her sides and shook her head wearily. 'I *have* to forget about him. But I'm finding it impossible. So it's important that I find something about him that makes me flinch. Something that tells me loud and clear that I would not be happy with him.'

'So we have an urgent need for potentially concealed flaws.' Jane frowned thoughtfully. 'Terrible kisser?'

'Incredible kisser.'

'Ah.' Jane looked interested. 'Do you want to expand on that?'

'No.' Lara gritted her teeth. 'I don't.'

Jane tapped her foot and thought hard. 'He's a workaholic. That's a definite flaw. You'd always be at the bottom of his list.'

'I like the fact that he's good with the patients and dedicated. I don't see it as a flaw.'

'You might when you're scraping his dinner into the bin every night.'

Lara shook her head miserably. 'No. It isn't good enough. Try again.'

'Too macho? He's quite cold and commanding. And he can be very sharp if someone screws up.'

'*You're* sharp if someone screws up,' Lara said dryly. 'It could have something to do with the fact that, if we screw up, someone can die.'

'Oh, well, I don't know!! I'm doing my best but finding flaws isn't my strength. If a man just looks at me I'm so bloody grateful I'm willing to overlook virtually everything! You're the one that sees nothing but flaws.' Jane looked at her with exasperation and then her brow cleared. 'Oh, I've got it. How could we have been so stupid? His flaw is his kids. You've already said that you can't get near him because they're always there. Taking on another woman's children would be a nightmare. All little girls read fairy-tales. You'd always be the wicked stepmother. They'd always resent you.'

Lara thought of the children and about how quiet Chloe was. She had no doubt that there were plenty of complicated emotions bubbling under the surface. 'You're right,' she said firmly. 'Never get involved with a man with kids. Asking for trouble.'

'Asking for trouble. Christian has more baggage than an airline.' Jane nodded decisively. 'That's the flaw. Now, focus on it and you'll go off him.'

'I hope so.'

For the sake of her sanity, she hoped so.

Lara was working in the paediatric casualty area the following morning when a mother stumbled in, carrying her toddler.

One look was all it took. 'Bring her straight into this room.' Directing them into Resus, Lara looked at the junior doctor who was reading a textbook at the desk. 'Could you ask Dr Blake to come and see this child, please?'

Penny put the book down. 'You do her obs and then I'll check her over and decide whether he needs to be—'

'Call him,' Lara ordered, her tone curt as she backed into Resus. She forgot about her own feelings—*forgot that she was trying to avoid him as much as possible.* 'Call him *now.*'

She hurried over, her heart sinking as she looked at the child, who seemed extremely agitated and poorly.

Hurry up, Christian.

'I'm just going to undress her, Mrs…' She glanced at the mother as she swiftly stripped the clothes from the toddler, leaving her in a vest and nappy. 'Sorry—I haven't even had a chance to ask your name.'

'Susan. Susan Wills. This is Amy. She was two in June.'

'And how long has Amy been ill? There, angel, we'll soon have you more comfortable.'

'Since yesterday afternoon, but she's only been bad

since this morning. She had diarrhoea and vomiting yesterday. And she keeps saying her tummy hurts.'

'Does she have any allergies?'

'Not that I know of.'

Lara checked the child's temperature. 'And has she been fully immunised?'

Penny walked into the room. 'I'm sure she has gastroenteritis,' she said confidently. 'There's a lot of it around.'

Lara bit her tongue. 'She's wheezing.'

'Is she asthmatic?' Penny reached for her stethoscope and the mother shook her head.

'She's only had breathing problems since yesterday.'

'Asthma does sometimes just develop at this age,' Penny murmured, and Lara reached for the paediatric wrap-around probe that would measure the child's oxygen saturation.

'I'm going to check her sats. I think she's hypoxic.'

Penny frowned. 'There are no signs of cyanosis.'

'But she's very agitated and that can be a sign of hypoxia in a child of this age. Is Dr Blake on his way?' Aware that the child needed urgent medical help, Lara studied the reading.

Penny gave a faint smile. 'Her sats look fine.'

'The reading isn't stable. You're looking at artefact.' Lara stroked a reassuring hand over the child's head. 'Try and keep still for me, sweetheart. There's a good girl.' She watched the number and then nodded. 'Ninety per cent. We need to give her some oxygen. She's tachycardic and pale and—'

'That can happen with any infection.' Penny washed her hands. 'Her breathing actually seems quite relaxed.'

Relaxed?

Knowing that to argue with Penny would achieve nothing except to frighten the mother, Lara was frantically considering her options when Christian strode through the door.

'You wanted me?'

'Yes.' Weak with relief, Lara reached for an oxygen mask. Christian would know what to do. 'She's pyrexial and she's making virtually no respiratory effort. I'm just going to give her some high-flow oxygen.'

'Good.'

'With a mask?' Penny frowned. 'She might find it easier to tolerate a nasal cannula.'

'Possibly, but the maximum flow rate is two litres a minute and she needs a higher concentration than that.' Lara gently placed the mask over the child's face. 'Do you like dressing up, Amy? This mask is exactly like a dressing-up mask.' She looked at Christian. 'She's been complaining of headache and abdominal pain.'

'It's highly probably that she has a GI infection and the headache is probably a result of dehydration,' Penny said crisply, reaching for an IV tray. 'A stomach bug. My flatmate has had the same thing all week.'

'That's quite possible. Or the abdominal pain could be referred from the diaphragm.' Lara held the mask in place and rubbed her finger gently against the child's cheek. 'You're a good girl. Dr Blake is just going to listen to your chest and feel your tummy.'

'Temperature?'

'Thirty-eight point seven and she's wheezing. She could be suffering from a lower respiratory tract infection.'

Penny looked at her. 'Pneumonia is extremely unlikely if there's wheeze present.'

'Her ears and throat are clear.' Christian examined the child's chest. 'Let's get a line in and take some bloods. They may not be conclusive but they might provide a useful baseline. We'll do the usual, plus CRP and ESR.'

The mother was white and upset. 'She kept complaining of a headache. I thought that was because of the temperature.'

'Mycoplasma?' Lara gave a tiny shrug and Christian looked at her as he removed the stethoscope from his ears.

'It's possible.' He tapped the child's chest, listening for dullness to percussion or bronchial breathing. 'There's no sign of consolidation,' he murmured, 'but that doesn't necessarily exclude pneumonia.'

'She has a rash, Christian,' Lara said quickly, noticing the red raised marks on the child's body.

'A rash?' the mother whimpered. 'Is it meningitis?'

Christian shook his head. 'I don't think that's what we're looking at here. Lara, give me a 22-gauge needle.' He stroked his hand along the child's arm, looking for a vein. 'Squeeze for me.'

Lara closed her fingers round the child's tiny wrist and Christian slid the needle into the vein with no apparent effort.

'That's quite a party trick,' Lara said, handing him some adhesive tape then reaching for the blood bottles that she'd put ready. Their movements were smooth and synchronised. 'Tell me what you want. FBC and cultures, obviously.'

He took the bottles from her and carefully withdrew the necessary blood. 'Viral titres and mycoplasma antibodies. I think you might be right.'

Penny walked back into the room with the radiographer just as Lara was bandaging the child's hand to a splint so that the cannula wouldn't be accidentally dislodged.

Christian glanced at the monitor. 'Her sats are still below ninety-two per cent. She's exhausted and she's going to need IV antibiotics so I'm going to call paediatric ICU.'

'PICU?' Penny looked startled and followed him out of

the room, clearly to glean more information on why he was so concerned.

Lara made the child more comfortable and explained what was happening to the mother.

The anaesthetist and the paediatrician arrived together, examined the child and transferred her to PICU.

Penny stared as they left the room with the child. 'Mycoplasma pneumonia? She had all the signs of gastroenteritis.'

'We won't know for sure until the results come back but clinically, yes, I'd say that Lara made a good guess.' Christian put the pen back into his pocket, his expression inscrutable. 'Fran rang through. Amy's father is in Reception. Can you go and talk to him, Lara? You're good with anxious relatives.'

It was obvious that he intended to speak to Penny and Lara quickly melted from the room, only too eager to follow his suggestion.

She took Mr Wills up to PICU and then returned to Paediatric Resus. There was no sign of Penny and Christian was at the desk, writing up some notes.

'I hope you directed her to the chapter on resuscitation of the sick child,' Lara muttered as she slid into the seat next to him.

Christian sat back in his chair. 'She didn't realise the child was so seriously ill.'

'I pointed it out.'

'Yes.' He gave a faint smile. 'She told me. She's very new to the ED. She hasn't yet worked out the nurses usually know more than the doctors.'

'I don't mind inexperience, but she didn't want to call you.' She stopped talking as Penny walked up to them.

'I had no idea that the child was so sick,' she said

humbly. 'I just thought she was quiet because she had a stomach bug. What was it that made you suspect that the child was seriously ill? I mean, you just took one look at her and took her into Resus and asked for Christian.'

Lara thought about it. 'I don't know.' Instinct? Experience? 'When you've seen a few sick children, you know when to worry.'

Penny pulled a face. 'I need to gain that instinct fast.'

'Work alongside Lara,' Christian suggested, rising to his feet in a fluid movement. 'She has the best instincts of any nurse I've worked with. It's a shame she's going to Australia.'

Lara watched as he strode from the room. *He was just complimenting her nursing skills,* she told herself. Nothing else.

And it wasn't a shame she was going to Australia.

It was the thing that was going to save her.

CHAPTER EIGHT

LARA lit the candles on the kitchen table and then blew them out again.

Too romantic.

Christian had made it all too clear that he wasn't interested in anything other than friendship. Since the kiss, he'd become even more detached and distant. At work he was cool and professional and he treated her exactly the same way as he treated the other nurses. At home, he spoke to her as if she was a valued friend.

He gave her no encouragement, barely glanced in her direction when they were together, and it was clear to her that he wasn't struggling with the situation in the same way that she was struggling.

Lara removed the plates from the cooker and stood for a moment, her mind drifting.

The kiss had obviously cured him of whatever attraction he'd felt.

Unfortunately it had had the opposite effect on her.

Lost in thought, Lara gave a start as she heard the sound of his key in the door and the plate slipped from her fingers.

'Stupid, stupid, stupid,' she muttered to herself as she stooped to pick up the broken pieces.

'Don't cut yourself.' Christian's deep voice came from the doorway and he walked towards her, a frown on his face. 'Was the plate wet?'

'No.' She kept her head down, afraid that her feelings would show in her expression. 'I just wasn't holding it properly. Sorry. It was expensive. I'll replace it.'

'Why would you want to replace it? It's only a plate.' He shrugged his broad shoulders out of his thick coat. 'It's freezing out there. We're going to have more snow. Are the girls asleep?'

'Yes.' She stood up, wrapped the broken pieces of plate and dropped them in the bin. 'They stayed awake as long as possible, waiting for you, but you were later than we all planned.'

'A group of teenagers drove into a lamppost half an hour before I was planning to leave. They weren't wearing seat belts.' Christian gave a rueful smile and poured himself a large whiskey. 'Can I offer you a drink?'

So formal. It was as if they were total strangers who'd never experienced an incredible, explosive kiss. 'No, thank you.' She finished laying the table. 'I'll just serve dinner and then I'll go to bed. I'm tired.'

Suddenly she wished she'd eaten with the children. It would have stopped her having to spend an uncomfortable evening with Christian.

'Don't just disappear.' He sat down on one of the kitchen chairs and stretched his legs out in front of him. 'You had a busy day.'

'Yes. That woman with the fractured femur took a long time to sort out.' She placed a dish of chicken in front of him. 'I hope you like spicy food. It has quite a lot of chilli in it.'

'I love spicy food. Are you all right?' He frowned across

at her as he served himself. 'Usually by this point in the evening you've cracked at least ten jokes. Are you ill?'

'No, not ill.'

In love.

The realisation struck her with the force of a tornado and she gave a soft gasp of shock. No. *No.* She couldn't be in love. Not now. Not with Christian.

Wrong man. Wrong time of her life.

Oh, help…

'Lara?' His eyes were fixed on her face, his expression curiously intent. 'What's the matter?'

'I've had a long day,' she mumbled, passing him a bowl of fluffy rice. 'Help yourself. It's getting cold.'

'You're not eating?'

'Yes. No. Just a small amount.' She was too shocked to eat. *Love?*

How had that happened? How could love just spring out of nowhere?

'What's wrong?' His voice was unexpectedly gentle. 'Are you missing your family?'

She gritted her teeth and wished he'd say something cutting and insensitive. *Anything that might help her cope with the fact that she was in love with a man who wasn't interested.* 'Yes, I miss them. No matter where we are or what we're doing, we've always managed to get together at Christmas. This is the first year that we've been spread out.'

'Tell me about your family Christmas. Did you have your own routines and traditions?'

Christmas. Routines and traditions.

It was as if the kiss had never happened. *As if they'd never shared an amazing moment of intimacy.*

Lara sat back, her plate untouched. 'Well, traditionally Christmas Eve was spent squashing presents so hard that

I almost broke them. Then I'd spend the whole night prising my brother's eyes open just to see if he was really asleep or just pretending. Then I'd get up at some unearthly hour when it was still dark and wake the whole household. Mum and Dad never minded. They'd make themselves a really strong pot of coffee and snuggle up together with us while we opened our stockings. Then we ate these amazing cinnamon biscuits shaped like stars that Mum only ever made at Christmas.'

'And how old were you then?' His voice was amused. 'Same age as Aggie?'

She pushed aside the sadness that threatened to swamp her. *Suddenly she felt strangely vulnerable and she wished that her family wasn't so far away.* 'Oh, I was at least twenty-four,' she joked lightly. 'I was describing last Christmas. So how about you? Tell me about your Christmas.'

'Much more formal than yours.' He helped himself to more chicken. 'On Christmas Eve my parents would hold a dinner for friends and colleagues of my father.'

'Colleagues?'

'He was a lawyer. He spent a great deal of time networking.'

Lara pulled a face. 'Christmas is for families.'

'Ah, that's where you're wrong.' He gave a mocking smile. 'In my family, Christmas is just another business opportunity. Get people while they're under the influence of champagne. But we did have a traditional lunch on Christmas Day.'

'Hold on.' Lara lifted a hand. 'When did you open your stocking?'

He shrugged. 'Whenever I liked. When I woke up.'

'Your parents didn't get angry if you woke them early?'

'I never woke them at all.' He finished the last of the chicken. 'I opened the stocking on my own.'

She was silent for a moment. 'That sounds lonely, Christian.'

'It was my life. I was an only child. Why aren't you eating?'

Lara glanced down at her plate and realised that it was still full. 'I—I suppose I'm just not hungry.'

She was too shocked by the discovery that she was in love. How could this have happened?

Her problem was *how* to love someone, not how *not* to love them.

She had absolutely no experience of this scenario. How was she supposed to handle it?

Would it just fade?

Would she eventually get on with her life and forget about him?

Or would she be in pain for ever?

'This one! This one!' Aggie danced up and down next to a huge Christmas tree and Christian raised his eyebrows.

'Aggie, that tree is enormous.'

'I know. I've never seen a tree like it. This tree is my *dream*.' Her eyes shone with excitement as she craned her neck to try and see the top. 'It's *perfect*.'

'I agree.' Lara stamped her feet to keep warm, her breath clouding the freezing air. *Love faded in time,* she told herself firmly, ignoring the dull ache in the centre of her chest. Australia would be the perfect distraction. 'How about you, Chloe? What do you think?'

'I— It's nice.' Chloe glanced anxiously towards her father. 'Do you think it's too big, Dad? We could pick a smaller one if you'd rather.'

Lara wondered why Chloe was always so anxious to please her father. *Say you like this one,* she urged silently as she glanced towards Christian. *She wants it but she's worried about you.*

He looked at Chloe and then looked at the tree. 'I think it's a great tree,' he said gruffly, and Lara smiled with relief.

He was a brilliant father. Whatever he thought, he had good instincts.

'That's decided, then.' She huddled into her scarf. 'Let's get on with it before we all freeze. We'll take the tree home, decorate it and I'll warm some mince pies in the oven. I can't believe how cold it is.'

'Do you think it might snow?' Aggie danced on the spot and Christian smiled.

'It doesn't often snow in London.'

Lara glanced up at the sky. It was grey and ominous. 'It could snow. It's cold enough.' And soon she'd be in Australia with her brother.

But the thought didn't bring the same rush of excitement that it had before she'd fallen in love.

'If it snows, we can make a snowman. Can we do the Rudolph Jive when we get home? And can you make us some of your amazing hot chocolate?' Aggie slipped her hand into Lara's and smiled up at her. 'With piles of chocolate and marshmallows. Ple-e-e-ease?'

'You want hot chocolate with mince pies? As long as you're not sick. I hate sick.'

Aggie giggled and hopped from one leg to the other. 'You can't hate sick. You're a nurse. Nurses are supposed to love sick.'

Lara shuddered dramatically. 'Trust me, I *hate* sick.'

Aggie stopped jumping and studied her with a frown on her face. 'You're *really* weird.' She hesitated and then smiled. 'But you're nice.' She skipped off to talk to Chloe and Lara stared after Aggie, a lump in her throat.

You're nice, too, she thought. *And I'm going to miss you.* Only she wasn't supposed to think that. She wasn't supposed to love Christian and she wasn't supposed to love his children.

None of this was supposed to have happened.

Everything was going horribly wrong.

Why, oh, why had she ever suggested moving in and helping with the children?

Why had she been so arrogant as to think that she'd be immune to a man as gorgeous as Christian Blake?

Feeling something approaching despair, she glanced towards him, only to find him studying her, molten heat simmering in his blue eyes.

'What? What's wrong?' Suddenly she didn't feel cold anymore. 'Why are you looking at me like that?' *He hadn't looked at her in that way since before the kiss.*

He shook his head slowly. 'I'm trying to work out how I can be violently attracted to a woman who can have a conversation about sick.'

His words took the breath from her body.

She'd assumed that he wasn't interested anymore

She'd assumed that the kiss had succeeded in killing off the chemistry for him.

But now it seemed as though he still felt the same way that she did.

Instinctively she glanced towards the children, but they were both busily examining the Christmas tree. '*Are* you violently attracted?'

'Do you doubt it?'

She kept her eyes on the children. 'I thought that you— you didn't seem— You've been very distant.'

'That was the idea. Unfortunately it doesn't seem to have worked.' His voice was steady. 'Keep talking about sick. With any luck I'll see sense sooner rather than later.'

'Seven-year-olds like talking about bodily functions.' Lara tried to keep her voice light but it was impossible because her heart was bumping so hard against her chest. *The chemistry was as powerful as ever.*

'This wasn't supposed to happen, Lara.'

'No.' Her voice was a breathless squeak. 'It wasn't. It hasn't. I mean…nothing's happened.'

His eyes dropped to her mouth. 'The kiss was a mistake. A big mistake.'

'I thought it hadn't bothered you.'

'Think again.'

She felt as though the breath had been punched from her lungs. 'I thought we both decided that we were going to forget about it.'

His gaze lifted and a sardonic gleam appeared in his eyes. 'This has proved to be the one occasion I regret the fact that I have an excellent memory. How about you? How's your forgetting going?'

'Funny you should bring that up.' She dragged her eyes away from his and watched while Aggie and Chloe took a closer look at the Christmas tree. 'Why is it that, when you're trying to forget something, that something becomes the only thing you can think about?'

'I don't know. I'm pondering the same question.'

'Perhaps we should try not forgetting it and then maybe we'd forget it.'

'Lara…' He closed his eyes and she whimpered.

'I know, I know. I'm making no sense. This can't be happening. I've never yet met a man who hasn't driven me to screaming pitch within three dates, and we haven't even been on *one*! It's all your fault. Show me a flaw, quickly. Reveal something positively shocking.'

'I didn't want this Christmas tree.' The first flakes of snow settled on his dark hair. With his cool, blue eyes and his dark jaw he looked impossibly handsome. 'Is that shocking?'

'No, it's sensible. The tree is far too big for your house. Actually, it's too big for anyone's house.' She studied it. 'It might look good in the middle of Leicester Square. Or maybe we could just ship it to the US. They'd have room for it out there. It's a big country.'

He raised his eyebrows. 'You said the tree was perfect.'

'It *is* perfect. Perfect for the children because they love it. But as for the rest of it…' She gave a helpless shrug and started to laugh, 'It's going to scratch the paint from your ceiling and you're going to be clearing up needles for months. And that's if we can even get it home. But it was worth buying it just to see their faces.'

He lifted a hand to his face and shook his head in disbelief. 'You're worse than the children.'

'Very possibly.'

'Why did I ever allow you to move in with me?' His tone was exasperated and she gave a helpless shrug.

'Because you were in a tight spot and we both thought we could easily resist each other. Obviously we were both a bit overconfident. Let's go home and decorate the tree. There's nothing quite like pine needles digging into your bottom to put a dent in the libido.'

He slipped his hand into his coat and removed his wallet. 'Chloe wouldn't have minded having a smaller one. We should have bought a smaller one.'

'I'm glad you didn't.' After a moment's hesitation she followed her instincts and slipped her arm through his.

'And Chloe wanted this one every bit as much as Aggie, but she didn't want to upset you.'

He stilled, a frown in his eyes. 'Why would she be afraid of upsetting me? Am I an ogre?'

'No, of course you're not.' Lara's smile faded. 'Perhaps she isn't afraid of upsetting you. I could be wrong. I haven't known her long. Perhaps she's just looking after you.'

'Possibly.'

But it was obvious that he thought it was something more than that and Lara resolved to engineer a way of talking to Chloe about something other than the usual mundane stuff.

'Daddy, it's snowing!' Shrieking with excitement. Aggie spread out her hands and lifted her face to the sky.

Watching the snowflakes drift gently onto the pavement, they made their way home and then hung lights on the tree and then decorations, including the ones that the girls had made with Lara.

'We baked them in the oven and painted them,' Aggie told Christian, staring in awe as her wonky star revolved slowly on the Christmas tree. 'Wow. It looks fantastic. Mummy never let us put our own decorations on the tree because she always said that matching silver ones looked better, but I don't think they do. This is much more fun.'

Chloe smiled as she hung her own version of a reindeer next to the star. 'It was fun,' she said shyly, 'making our own decorations. Thank you, Lara. And I love my new bedroom.'

'Good.'

Lara glanced at Chloe, puzzled. She was just too polite. She was twelve years old. Almost a teenager and yet she never did anything wrong. She didn't fight with her sister. She didn't argue or stamp or even roll her eyes. What was going on? Suddenly Lara wished that the child would do something that required at least a mild rebuke. Anything that would make it seem less likely that she was bottling up something enormous. 'I'm going to heat up those mince pies we made. Will you help me, Chloe?'

'Of course.' Chloe hung the last of the decorations on her side of the tree and walked towards the kitchen with Lara. 'Just mince pies?'

'I think so. We only had lunch a few hours ago.' Lara stooped to lift the mince pies out of the oven. 'So when is the school disco, Chloe?'

'It's next Saturday.' Chloe took a plate from the cupboard. 'But I'm not going.'

'Why aren't you going?'

'Because it doesn't finish until ten o'clock. That's too late.'

'Too late for what?' Lara slid the mince pies onto the plate. 'You're not usually asleep until then and it's the holidays. What's the problem?'

'I don't want Dad to have to come and pick me up.'

'Why not?' Lara put milk on to boil and placed mugs on a tray. 'He wouldn't mind.'

Chloe shook her head. 'It's too much to ask.'

Lara stood still. 'Chloe, he's your father. His role is to ferry you everywhere at all sorts of inconvenient hours. *You're not supposed to be this thoughtful!*'

'I don't want to be a bother. He's had a lot to cope with.'

'Does he look as though he's struggling?'

'No, but he only ever thinks about work and us. Never about himself.'

Lara rescued the milk from the hob and made the chocolate. 'Stop thinking about him and think about yourself. Would you like to go to the disco?'

Chloe didn't look at her. 'No. I'll stay here.'

No, you won't, Lara thought to herself as she lifted the tray and carried it through to the living room. *One way or another, Cinderella, you will be going to the ball.*

Christian checked that both girls were asleep and then strolled downstairs to the sitting room.

The Christmas tree lights glowed brightly and the log fire flickered and crackled in the grate. The remains of the game that Aggie had been playing was still strewn over the rug.

The room felt lived in and cosy.

Lara was lying on the sofa, her eyes closed, but she opened them when he walked into the room. 'Sorry.' She gave a faint smile. 'Just feeling mildly exhausted.'

'Full-time employment and children aren't a relaxing combination.'

She gave him a long look and then sat up. 'Absolutely. Well, I suppose I'd better go to bed.'

'Running away, Lara?' Part of him hoped that she was. It would make things so much easier.

Her gaze slid to his. 'Perhaps I am. I don't know what else to do and I've tried all the other alternatives. The tension is making my stomach churn and I've never felt like this before. I don't want to feel this way about you. I need you to reveal a really major flaw very quickly.'

'I have dozens of major flaws.'

Lara looked at him with something close to desperation. 'I can't see any of them.'

Christian examined the contents of his glass. 'My ex-wife called me a cold-hearted bastard who was incapable of making an emotional connection. Does that help?'

'No. Because I've seen you with your girls. You're wonderful with them. And you're great with worried children in the ED. Not cold at all.'

'Children are different,' he said softly. 'They have no artifice, no hidden agenda.'

'Did your wife have a hidden agenda?'

He stilled. 'I couldn't give her what she wanted. You need to remember that, Lara. It might be just the flaw you're looking for.'

'So because the two of you were incompatible, you're never going to get involved with a woman again? Has it occurred to you that it isn't a good example to set? Just because it went wrong once in the past, it doesn't mean it can't go right in the future.'

'From that comment I take it that your parents are extremely happily married.'

'Thirty years last June. Why? Are yours divorced now?'

'Oh, no. Nothing so civilised.' He drained his glass, feeling the warmth from the alcohol spread through his veins. 'They preferred to stay together and fight.'

'Oh. Well, I suppose that helps explain why you've managed to create such a lovely stable home for your children.'

'Have I? They have one parent.'

'One *loving* parent.'

'It isn't what I wanted for them.' He hesitated, unsure just how much to reveal. 'When Fiona left, the girls were torn apart with insecurity. She hadn't ever even spent much time with them but that seemed only to make things worse. They believed that they were the reason that she left. They knew she hated being a mother.'

Lara winced. 'She couldn't have hated it that much. She had two children.'

Christian stared into the bottom of his glass. 'I don't think she ever thought it through. People don't, always. Society expects a woman to be maternal. The last thing she said to me before she left was something like, "You wanted these children, well, it's your turn to look after them."' He gave a short laugh. 'The irony was that she never had looked after them. She employed nannies all the way through and I accepted that because I could see that she needed her work.'

'Do you miss her?'

Christian felt the tension across his shoulders. 'I feel bad for the girls. When your children are hurting, it's impossible not to ask yourself if you could have done something differently.'

'Like what?'

'I don't know.' It was the first time he'd ever spoken his thoughts aloud. 'But there must have been something more I could have done to have stopped her leaving.'

'You obviously loved her very much.'

Christian stared at her, wondering how she'd managed to come to that conclusion. 'There was no love between us at all,' he said flatly. 'And that was the problem. Love is the one thing you can't manufacture. Everything else can be bought if the money is there. Houses, nannies, good schools—they're all available for a price, but love—no.'

'You didn't love her?'

Was he supposed to deny the truth?

Christian nursed his empty glass, wondering whether to fill it again. 'I thought I did,' he said finally. 'But I was wrong. I married her for the wrong reasons.'

'Did she love you?'

Why the hell was he telling her this? With a determined effort he put the glass down on the mantelpiece. He didn't need a headache and he didn't need to indulge in maudlin confessions. 'She loved my money.'

'I'm sure there was more to it than that,' Lara said softly. 'You have a lot of very special qualities, Christian.'

'I thought you were searching for flaws.'

She gave a weak smile. 'Yes. Thanks for reminding me. Did your wife stay at home when the children were little?'

'Fiona was working on her laptop in the delivery room, thirty minutes after Aggie was born.' *While he'd been busy falling in love with his daughter.*

'But if she didn't want to be a mother…'

'Why did she have the children?' He gave a twisted smile. 'For me. She knew I wanted to create a stable family. If she'd confessed that she didn't want children, I never would have married her.'

'They must have been in a state when she left.'

'For six months Aggie slept in my bed because she was afraid that, if she didn't, I'd leave, too, when she was asleep.' His voice was gruff. 'And Chloe—well, she said less but she was hollow-eyed and listless. We stumbled on together and eventually we somehow managed to form ourselves into a family again. It's starting to work. I can't risk destabilising that.'

Lara looked at him. 'You're assuming that they'd be hurt if you had another relationship. But maybe they wouldn't be.'

There was a long, difficult silence while Christian struggled against the masculine instincts that threatened to drive common sense out of his brain. 'Maybe not.' His tone was rough. 'But that's a risk I'm not prepared to take.'

CHAPTER NINE

'How high was the wall, Eddie?' Lara checked the young man's observations and recorded them on the chart.

'Higher than I thought it was, thanks to the contents of a bottle of champagne.' The young man shifted on the trolley, the pain making him wince. 'Must have been about four metres, I suppose. I feel as though my entire body has snapped in half.'

'Hopefully it won't be that bad—' Lara's smile was sympathetic '—but we will need to take some X-rays. I'll ask a doctor to come and see you now.'

She stepped towards the door just as Christian entered. 'Did I hear you mention the fact that you need a doctor?'

Lara felt her heart rate double and quickly turned away from him. *It was becoming harder and harder to work with him and act normally.*

Flaws, she reminded herself. She needed to fall out of love with him and the only way to do that was to find his flaws.

'Lara?' His soft prompt brought her back from fantasyland to reality.

'This is Eddie,' she said, tucking her pen back into her pocket and trying to concentrate on her job. 'He jumped off a wall.'

'We were coming out of a restaurant after our Christmas lunch,' Eddie groaned, lifting his hand to his head. 'I'm in a lot of pain. I thought alcohol was supposed to numb the senses.'

'We'll give you something for that right now,' Lara said, reaching for an X-ray form and swiftly filling in the blank spaces while Christian examined his patient.

'Don't move me around too much, my head is spinning. Why are you looking at my spine?' Eddie grumbled as he followed Christian's smooth instructions and moved on the trolley to facilitate a fuller examination. 'It's my feet that are killing me.'

Lara wandered back to the trolley. 'If you land on both heels you can damage more than your feet,' she explained. She turned to Christian. 'Do you want him on his front so that you can examine his Achilles tendon?'

'In a minute. I'll just look at his ankles and feet first.' He examined the man's heels and Lara noticed the swelling and obvious bruising.

'Ow, that hurts!' Eddie flinched backwards and Christian murmured an apology.

'You've very tender over the calcaneum.'

'I don't know my calcaneum from my cranium but I do know that I'm in bloody agony and I'm never drinking again. If I hadn't had so much champagne I would have known that the wall was too high. It's just that I thought I could fly.'

Lara caught Christian's eye and tried not to laugh.

'I need you to lie on your front, Eddie,' he said, 'so that I can examine your Achilles tendon.'

Lara helped Eddie manoeuvre onto his front. 'Wriggle down a bit so that your feet dangle over the end. That's it. Perfect.'

Christian gently squeezed the mid-calf, looking for

normal plantar flexion of the ankle. 'That's fine. If you can turn over again, Eddie. I'm just going to send you for some X-rays. Can I have a form, Lara?'

Lara handed him the form that she'd already completed. 'Sign on the dotted line.' She grinned at him. 'Calcaneal X-rays—both feet. Is there anything I've missed?'

'I doubt it.' He scanned the form and signed, a trace of humour in his eyes as he glanced at her. 'You don't usually miss anything, do you? I'm starting to think you're a mind-reader, Staff Nurse King.'

'It's called anticipation and it just means that I've worked here for too long. If I hang around any longer I'll be able to treat the patients before they've even had the accident.' Lara took the signed form from him and put the side up on the trolley. 'I'm locking you in, Eddie, just in case you get any more bright ideas about jumping and flying. Hold on tight. You and I are going to take a trip down to X-Ray.'

She left Eddie with the radiographer and went in search of Jane, who was checking the controlled drugs. 'Emergency meeting needed.'

'Not when I'm counting ampoules of morphine.' Jane finished the task, dismissed the staff nurse who had been helping her and turned to Lara. 'Well?'

'I need a new flaw.'

'What's wrong with the old one?' Jane locked the drug cupboard. 'The man has two demanding children. I thought we agreed that they are *enormous* flaws.'

'We did. But they're not.' Lara slumped against the wall. 'I love them.'

'You love his kids?' Jane pinned the keys into her pocket. 'Lara, you're in trouble.'

'I know, I know. But they're so sweet. To be honest, it would be impossible not to love them.'

'That's because they're still on their best behaviour and they don't know you have dishonourable designs on their father. Once they work it out, they'll turn into horribly, snivelling flaws,' Jane predicted in a dark tone, but Lara shook her head.

'I'm not sure that they will. You have to think of something else.'

'No, *you* have to think of something else. Some*one* else, to be precise. Christian Blake isn't for you.' Jane's voice was serious. 'You're going to get hurt.'

'I can't believe you're saying that! You were the one who thought I should have a fling!'

'A fling, yes. A lifetime of agony because you've fallen in love with a guy who isn't interested in a relationship, no. That isn't what I wanted for you.'

'How do you know I'm in love with him?'

'Because I know you.'

Lara breathed out heavily. 'Why is it that I can never meet anyone I even remotely like and then finally when I meet someone that turns my whole life upside down, he's got two children and he isn't interested?'

'And you have a ticket to Australia,' Jane reminded her. 'A month ago you were excited about going. You need to get away and stop deluding yourself. Go and sit on Bondi Beach and look at some half-naked Australian men. They should take your mind off Christian.'

Lara looked at her, unconvinced. 'Yes. I'll do that.'

What choice did she have?

'There's a reduction in Bohler's angle.' Christian stared at Eddie's X-ray on the light box, trying not to be aware of Lara by his side. *She smelt fantastic.* 'It's a sign of compression.'

It took her a moment to respond and, when he glanced

at her, he saw that her expression was vacant. *What was she thinking?* 'Lara?'

She gave a little start and peered at the X-ray. 'Oops. Well, I suppose that's what you get when you drink a bottle of champagne and misjudge your landing.'

Eddie sighed. 'Is it bad?

Christian turned away from the light box. 'We need to refer you to the orthopaedic team. They'll decide how best to handle you but they're going to want to admit you.'

The man closed his eyes. 'Merry Christmas, Eddie.'

'It's not as bad as all that.' Lara walked across to him and gave him a sympathetic smile. 'Hospitals are fun places to be at Christmas.'

'Really?'

'Actually, no. It's a myth that hospitals are fun. Everyone who is well enough goes home so the only people left are very sick.' Her eyes twinkled. 'And then there are the patients…'

Eddie laughed but Christian found himself unable to drag his gaze from Lara, *unable to look away from the dimple at the corner of her mouth.* It appeared every time she smiled and that was most of the time. He loved her irrepressible sense of humour.

And she was wonderful with patients.

She had a natural feel for how to handle each case and modified her behaviour accordingly. When the patient was seriously injured she was calm and reassuring, but when the injuries were less serious she had a light-hearted touch that never failed to make patients laugh.

She was the most talented nurse he'd ever worked with. *And she kissed like a man's hottest fantasy.*

Was he doing the right thing, resisting the chemistry?

A thud of lust threatened to destroy his self-control and he gritted his teeth. He pulled the X-rays out of the light box and slid them back into the brown envelope. 'The orthopaedic team are on their way down to see you now.'

'Is there anyone you want me to phone?' Lara took a pad out of her pocket. 'Girlfriend? Mother? Boss? Santa?'

Eddie pulled a face. 'Unfortunately for my promotion prospects, my boss was there when I jumped so you don't need to call him. For goodness' sake, don't call my mother because I'll never hear the last of it. I suppose you could call my girlfriend, although she won't be too pleased, either. She had plans for Christmas.'

Lara grinned. 'I'll call your girlfriend now and with any luck she'll arrive in time to hear what the orthopods have to say about you.'

Christian watched as she walked out of the room.

'That nurse is gorgeous,' Eddie said dreamily. 'Is she married? Because I'm going to be looking for a new girlfriend once my current model gets wind of what I've done.'

Christian felt a sudden rush of heated anger envelop him. 'I don't think she's married.' *Why did he care if another man was interested in Lara?* It wasn't as if he was in a position to have a relationship with her. He didn't want to risk shattering his children's fragile sense of security.

He walked back into the main area of the ED and immediately bumped into Lara. He reached out a hand to steady her, wondering why fate was so intent on tormenting him. Why couldn't he have bumped into Jane or Fran?

'Sorry. I wasn't looking where I was going.' He released her immediately and noticed her take a step backwards.

So it wasn't just him, then.

'I just called Eddie's girlfriend. She's on her way in. She sounded immensely irritated to think he was here.' Her mouth curved into a smile but her eyes were shadowed and tired. 'Do you think we should call Security? He might need protection.'

Christian studied her delicate bone structure and the tiny freckles that dusted her nose. Eddie was right. She *was* beautiful. He wondered why she was tired. Was looking after the house and the girls too much for her?

Or was she lying awake at night, suffering as he was?

'Eddie expressed an interest in your marital status.'

Lara lifted a hand. 'Oh, no.' She shook her head. 'I can see his flaws without even going on a date. He obviously drinks too much and his spatial awareness must be pretty poor if he couldn't judge the distance to the ground. Disaster. If we went out for dinner, I'd strangle him before we reached the end of the first course.'

'Has any man ever come close to meeting your impossibly high standards?'

Why had he asked that question?

She was obviously wondering the same thing because the laughter in her eyes faded and she looked away, clearly self-conscious. 'No. Absolutely not. Never.'

A tense silence followed her statement and Christian felt the slow throb of his heartbeat. 'Lara—'

'I forgot to mention,' she interrupted him quickly, her tone unnaturally bright, 'both the girls want to go to sleep-overs tomorrow night. It's with friends that they've played with before so I'm assuming that's all right with you. I'll send in a bag for them and they can go straight from school. It's quite convenient, actually, because we have a bit of a staffing crisis on the nursing front and I've promised Jane that I'll do a night shift.'

Christian felt an immediate rush of tension. 'I'm doing a night shift, too.'

Something flickered in her eyes. 'Oh. Right. Well, that's—that's…'

'That's what?'

She gave a funny twisted smile. 'Another test of self-control?'

Christian felt a hot flame of lust burn through his body. 'It will be fine. We'll both be working.'

'Of course we will. Just make sure there's no mistletoe.' She backed away from him. 'Well, I'll just go and break the news to Eddie that his girlfriend is on her way. Judging from her tone of voice, he might want to try and run away on two broken feet.'

Another heavy fall of snow brought chaos to the roads and the night was frantically busy.

'Why don't people just go to bed when it gets dark?' Lara said desperately as she called the medical ward to try and hasten the transfer of two patients so that they could make room in the department.

'This is why we don't usually work nights,' Jane said, juggling a pile of X-rays. 'There's never any chance to rest. Ambulance Control just rang. They're bringing in a young guy who's been stabbed. Can you go into Resus?'

'My favourite place.'

'I don't know why you're complaining.' Jane tucked the X-rays under her arm. 'Pretty soon you'll be sunning yourself in Sydney and this will all be a distant memory.'

'Yes.' *Why did that option no longer sound exciting? She wanted to see her brother, but as for the rest of it…*

Wondering why she'd suddenly lost all her bounce and energy, Lara joined the team in Resus and worked on automatic, relying on experience to carry her through.

She wasn't going to look at Christian more than was absolutely necessary.

She wasn't going to admire him.

'He's arrested.' Penny's voice rose slightly. 'There's

blood everywhere. They must have hit his heart when they stabbed him. The cardiothoracic team are waiting for him in Theatre.'

'He isn't going to make it to Theatre,' Christian said grimly. 'Start external chest compressions. Lara, get me a thoracotomy pack.'

Penny's face was white as she followed his instructions. 'You're going to open his chest *here*?'

'He's arrested,' Christian said bluntly. 'We're not exactly overwhelmed with options.'

As Lara scrubbed and put on a gown, she glanced towards Penny and wondered whether she'd ever witnessed severe trauma before. 'You're doing really well, Penny,' she said quickly, opening the pack for Christian and handing him gloves, a face shield and an apron. 'I've called blood transfusion.'

'Good. Let's hope he's going to need it.' Christian moved to the patient's left side and lifted his arm. 'Stop chest compressions, Penny.' Without hesitation he made an incision in the left chest wall.

Lara handed him a rib retractor and adjusted the light. 'Is that better?'

'All I can see is blood.' His fingers swift and decisive, Christian widened the incision. 'I can see the pericardium—it's bulging.'

Hoping that Penny wasn't going to faint into the wound, Lara watched as he skillfully evacuated the blood from the pericardial sac.

'Right—now I just need to work out what's going on here…' He put a finger over the defect and performed internal cardiac massage. 'Lara, give me a prolene suture.'

She ripped open the appropriate packet and he took it

swiftly and worked to repair the damage to the heart. 'The knife must have gone straight between his ribs.'

'Yes.' Christian paused and glanced at the monitor. 'Check cardiac rhythm and output.'

'He's in VF.'

'Give me the internal defibrillation paddles.' Without hesitation, Christian placed a paddle either side of the heart and delivered the shock.

'He has a pulse,' Lara murmured. 'Gosh. It's our lucky night. More Christmas miracles.'

'Lucky?' Penny looked at her, her face white. 'How can you call him lucky?'

'Because if Christian hadn't opened his chest, he'd be dead now.' Lara was still watching the monitor. 'Do you want to put in a catheter?'

'Yes, and an arterial line.' Christian looked at Penny. 'We need to check his bloods again. U and Es, FBCs, glucose and clotting. And give him 1.5 grams of cefuroxime.'

Penny didn't answer and Lara glanced towards her. The young doctor's face was ashen.

Noticing her sway slightly, Lara dropped a pair of forceps on the floor. 'Oops. Silly me.' Her voice was calm. 'Do you mind picking that up for me, Penny? Just put them on the side, over there.'

The action of stooping to retrieve the forceps restored the blood to Penny's head and, when she straightened and put the forceps down, she had some colour in her cheeks. She gave Lara a hesitant smile of thanks, clearly aware that Lara's sudden display of 'clumsiness' had been intentional.

Christian was still involved with the patient and hadn't noticed anything amiss.

'It's jolly hot in here,' Lara murmured. 'Why don't you go out and take a breath of fresh air, Penny?'

Christian lifted his head and frowned but at that moment the cardiothoracic team strode into the room and the focus of his attention shifted. 'Gregg.' He nodded to his colleague. 'We have a patient for you.'

The cardiothoracic surgeon walked up to the trolley and Lara took advantage of the extra staff to give Penny a little push.

'Someone else can take those bloods. You go outside and breathe. Then go to the staffroom and have a cup of tea.'

Penny didn't argue and Lara turned back to the patient who was now in the hands of the cardiothoracic team.

'Nice work, Christian. If you ever want a job, just pick up the phone.'

They stabilised the patient sufficiently to move him and then Lara went to find Penny. There was no sign of her but she found Jane instead.

'Have you seen Penny? She looked a bit sick. I wanted to check on her.'

'I'm not surprised she looked sick,' Jane said calmly. 'I just put my head round the door in Resus and it looked as though you'd slaughtered a goat. Not very tidy, are you?'

Lara bristled. 'We saved that man's life—well, so far, anyway.'

'Next time try and keep at least some of the blood *inside* the patient.' Jane gave a faint smile. 'You did well. You and Christian are an amazing team. And don't worry about Penny. I've already seen her. I talked to her and then sent her home.'

'You did?'

'Yes. She thought you were very kind. But she was very traumatised, as you rightly guessed.'

Lara sighed. 'I don't think the pace of the ED suits her. She finds it all too stressful.'

'It is stressful.' Jane gave a philosophical smile. 'I'll talk to Christian about her at some point, see what he thinks.' She picked up a pile of files and handed them to Lara. 'Do you mind taking these to Christian? He's in his office and he was asking for them earlier. It's the next job on my long list. And tell him that Penny has gone home. I'll give him the details tomorrow.'

Lara opened her mouth to say that she didn't want to go and see Christian in his office, but Jane had already left the room.

Gritting her teeth, Lara clutched the files. Apart from the inevitable demands of Resus, she'd been avoiding him all night. She really didn't want to see him outside the clinical situation.

But delivering files was hardly a problem, was it? She'd just put them on his desk and leave.

Trying to ignore the banging of her heart, Lara walked to Christian's office. The door was open but the only light came from a flickering computer screen.

Why was he sitting in the dark?

'Jane said that you're waiting for these.' She put the files on his desk. 'And she wants you to know that Penny has gone home.'

'Why has she gone home?'

The sound of his voice sent wicked, sensual heat curling through her pelvis. 'Because she wasn't feeling a hundred per cent. I think she was feeling a bit off colour when we were in Resus.' The darkness created a dangerous intimacy and Lara started to back towards the door.

'I wondered why you were sending her out of the room. I didn't notice that she was off colour.'

'You were opening a patient's chest at the time so you have a decent excuse for not noticing. But that probably won't stop her thinking that we're cold and unfeeling.'

He was silent for a moment. 'Are we cold and unfeeling, Lara?'

'You just saved a man's life, Christian,' Lara said softly. 'How can you even ask that question?'

He studied her, his eyes glittering in the semi-darkness. 'Working in the ED distorts your view of life, don't you think?'

'Yes,' she said honestly, 'I think it probably does.'

'Is that why you're going to Australia? Because you want to return to normal life? Are you tired of living your life along the edge of other people's disasters?'

Her heart banged against her chest as she searched vainly for the answer to his question. *She didn't know why she was leaving anymore.*

'It seemed like a good idea at the time, but that was before—' She stopped in mid-sentence and he rose to his feet and walked across to her.

'Before what, Lara?'

Silence enclosed them and then he reached behind her and shut the door, turning the key in the lock with a purposeful movement. 'Before—what?'

Why had he locked the door?

'Before I walked into your office, holding mistletoe. Before I moved in with you. I don't know.' Her voice was a whisper in the darkness. 'Sometimes when I'm working in Resus I remember that life is short and unpredictable. No one knows that more than we do. You have to make the most of every single bit of happiness that comes your way. But I understand that you don't want to do that. I know how much you worry about upsetting your girls.'

He was standing so close to her that the tension was almost unbearable and suddenly she knew she had to get away from him while she was still in possession of a grain of willpower.

She turned swiftly and put her hand on the key, but his hand covered hers, warm and strong.

For a moment they just stood like that and then his fingers tightened and she turned slowly to look at him. His face was close to hers and she saw in the depths of his blue eyes that he was fighting the same battle that she was. A war between sheer animal attraction and cold common sense.

Then he gently slid his hand round the back of her neck and drew her towards him, lowering his mouth to hers.

The slow, erotic skill of his kiss sparked an explosion of excitement so shockingly intense that she felt a sudden rush of heat through her body that threatened to melt her bones.

He cupped her face with his hands, holding her firmly as he silenced her shocked moan with the heat and demands of his mouth.

It was a kiss like no other she'd ever experienced and for a suspended moment in time she was unable to think or move, *unable to do anything except react in the most primitive way.*

The heat of the kiss intensified until he lifted her into his arms in one easy movement and carried her across to his desk.

Without breaking the kiss—*as if the taste of her mouth was essential to give him life*—he knocked papers and files onto the floor with an impatient sweep of his arm and then placed her on the desk.

Lara lifted her hands to his shoulders, feeling the hard swell of muscle and the strength and power of his body.

The tension that had been building for weeks exploded between them and with a frantic movement she slid her hands up inside his scrub suit, feeling warm male flesh under her desperately seeking fingers. With a low groan he slid his hands down her trembling thighs, pushed them apart and hauled her hard against him.

'*Christian...*' The shock of the contact stole the breath from her body and she gave a little sob as she felt the hard press of his arousal through the thin fabric of his scrub suit.

'I need you naked. I need you naked *now*.' He groaned the words against her mouth, breaking the contact only to jerk her top over her head. It landed in a soft heap and her bottoms followed moments later.

Tortured by excitement, Lara felt his fingers slide over her arms and then her bra was gone too and his mouth finally moved from her lips to her breast.

The slow graze of his tongue against her nipple sent shock waves through her system and she writhed against him, struggling to ease the growing ache deep in her pelvis.

She felt desperate, completely desperate, and he was obviously aware of that fact because she felt his warm, seeking fingers move lower until he was touching her intimately.

His skilled caress drove her past the point where restraint or common sense might have intervened and, when he brought his mouth back to hers, lightning heat and molten excitement poured through her body. She slid her own hands down over his warm, hard flesh and lower still, the sheer intensity of her need making her bold.

'Please, Christian, please...' She whimpered the words against his mouth and her fingers closed around the warm, pulsing strength of his arousal.

He stilled and she felt his last desperate struggle for control.

She heard his harsh breathing, felt the tension in his powerful frame, and knew that, if he stopped now, she'd die for sure.

She slid her hips closer to his and wrapped her legs

around him, her trembling, aroused body delivering a blatant invitation that he met with his own fierce demands.

His mouth found hers again and then she felt his hands on her hips, easing her forward. And then he was inside her, driving deep with a series of smooth thrusts that sent more shock waves spiralling through her thoroughly overexcited body.

She climaxed immediately, her body in the grip of an explosion of sensation that allowed her no breathing space.

'Lara…' He muttered her name against her mouth, sliding a hand over her bottom to bring her closer still, and the intimacy was so perfect—so deliciously shocking—that she clung to him, afraid to let go.

The feel of his body joined with hers was so amazing that another climax devoured her immediately and this time her uninhibited response tore through his own control and she felt the sudden increase in masculine thrust as he reached his own completion.

It was terrifying and exhilarating and she clung to his shoulders, overwhelmed by the intensity of the experience, struggling to regain her breath.

Gradually the sensations eased and she became aware of her surroundings. The flickering computer screen next to them, the few papers that hadn't been knocked from the desk in the frantic pursuit of passion.

They'd made love in his office.

With a moan of disbelief she tried to draw away from him but he held her, his face buried in her neck as he breathed in her scent. Finally he lifted his head and his eyes met hers.

'Lara—'

'Don't say anything.' She didn't want him to say anything because words could only spoil the perfection of what they'd just shared.

He withdrew from her gently and reached down to retrieve her clothes. With gentle hands he replaced her bra and slipped her top over her head. 'Are you sorry?'

She slid her legs into her trousers and pushed her hair away from her face. 'How could I be sorry?' She spoke in a whisper even though they were alone in his office. 'It was perfect.'

'Yes. It was.' His voice was deep. 'That's why I thought you might be sorry.'

So it had been perfect for him, too.

Impulsively she turned to him, overwhelmed by emotion that she didn't understand. 'What if I didn't go travelling? What if I just visited my brother and then came straight home? I could look after the girls and we could—'

'Don't.' He groaned the words against her mouth. 'Don't say that. You know that isn't an option. The girls can't cope with any more changes. Their lives need to be stable and predictable.'

'But I love the girls. We could make it work.' Consumed by a misery that she didn't understand, she looked at him. 'We have something special, Christian.'

'Yes.' He stilled. 'But you have no idea how traumatised they were when their mother left. It just isn't something I can risk again.'

'I wouldn't hurt them, Christian.'

'Not intentionally, no.' He moved away from her as if he didn't trust himself not to touch her again. 'But I don't intend to make a habit of having women walking in and out of their lives.'

Was it possible to experience perfect happiness and the depths of misery almost simultaneously? 'So that's it?'

He ran a hand over his face and turned away from her. 'It has to be.' His tone was bleak. 'It has to be, Lara.'

CHAPTER TEN

'I CAN'T see her,' Chloe whispered as the three of them craned their necks to see Aggie on the stage. 'She's supposed to come on after the Kings. Where is she?'

Christian stared at the stage and tried to control his reaction to Lara, who was sitting right beside him. She was avoiding his gaze but he knew that she was every bit as aware of him as he was of her.

Their moment of passion had stripped back his self-control and he just wanted to haul her into a dark cave and keep her there.

'Oh, my goodness, they all look so sweet,' Lara murmured as a line of young children shuffled onto the stage in various muddy-coloured robes. 'I've never actually been to a school nativity play before. It's amazing.'

She was amazing, he thought, coming to watch his daughter in her nativity play. Especially after what had happened between them.

He wouldn't have blamed her if she'd packed her bags and walked away.

But she hadn't done that. She'd just carried on with her life—working and helping him with the girls. She was a little paler and possibly a little less bouncy, but she was still Lara.

'Dad!' Chloe nudged him. 'You're not concentrating.'

Forcing his mind away from Lara, Christian scanned the line of children on the stage. 'Why are they all wearing stripy teatowels on their heads?'

'Because they're shepherds.' Smiling, Lara glanced towards him, but her smile faded almost instantly.

'I love the woolly sheep,' Chloe murmured, and Lara dragged her eyes away from his and back to the stage.

Christian felt a sudden rush of tension engulf him. *They couldn't even behave naturally anymore.*

'I can see Aggie.' Lara moved slightly in her seat and waved her hand.

'Don't wave,' Chloe muttered. 'The teachers tell them off if they wave.'

'Sorry.' Lara clasped her hands in her lap. 'It's just that she looks gorgeous.'

Aggie walked onto the stage in her white angel costume, her eyes frantically searching for Christian.

She saw him and gave a dazzling smile, happier and more confident than she'd been for months, and suddenly he felt a lump in his throat. *How could he doubt that he was doing the right thing? How could he ever consider putting his needs before those of his girls?*

'Go, baby,' he murmured, and Lara pulled a face and started to chew her nails.

'I'm really nervous for her,' she whispered. 'We've been practising her lines all week.'

Christian reached across and gently removed her hand from her mouth. 'Stop biting your nails. She only says one sentence.'

'I know.' Deprived of her nails, Lara bit her lip instead. 'We've practised it over and over again. I hope she gets it right.'

Christian watched his daughter but he was acutely aware of Lara sitting next to him, mouthing the words along with Aggie.

She was sweet with his children.

Touched by how much she appeared to care, he gritted his teeth and reminded himself that it didn't make any difference. Liking his children was quite different from taking them on for the rest of her life.

Sweat broke out on his brow.

Where had that thought come from?

There had never been any suggestion of permanence in his relationship with Lara.

They'd rejected a wild affair, nothing more.

Clearly unaware of his thoughts, Lara was clapping. 'Wasn't Aggie great, Chloe?'

Chloe gave a wistful smile. 'Yes,' she said huskily. 'She was tremendous.'

Something in Chloe's tone drew Christian's attention and for a moment he forgot about Lara. Was Chloe jealous of Aggie? It had never crossed his mind before, but still…

Realising that the nativity play had ended, he clapped dutifully.

Christian noticed that quite a few of the other parents were glancing at Lara with interest.

She had clearly noticed the same thing because she blushed slightly.

'Oh, dear. The gossips will be working overtime,' she said to Christian as she slipped her coat on and reached for her bag. She held the scarf across her mouth and nose, gave him a sultry look and adopted a foreign accent. '"Oo is zee mysterious and glamorous woman seen out with zee handsome Christian Blake?"'

'I don't know—who is she?' Trying to lighten the

atmosphere, Christian pretended to look around him and Chloe chuckled.

'Dad! You're awful. Lara looks gorgeous. Surely you can see that.'

Yes, unfortunately he could see that.

Had his daughter noticed, too?

Was that why she was so quiet?

Chloe was growing up. Perhaps she'd picked up the tension between him and Lara.

He reached for Chloe's hand. 'You both look gorgeous.' He smiled at his daughter. 'What do you want to do when we've collected Aggie?'

Chloe's smile was self-conscious. 'I don't mind. Anything.'

'Actually, I thought Chloe and I might go shopping,' Lara said casually, wrapping the scarf around her neck and glancing at her watch. 'The shops don't close until late.'

'What are we shopping for?'

'A new outfit for the school disco.' Lara smiled at Chloe. 'I've seen an amazing dress. It would look great on you.'

Chloe shook her head. 'I'm not going to the school disco.'

Christian frowned. 'I'd forgotten about it. When is it?'

'It doesn't matter,' Chloe said quickly. 'I'm not going. It's fine. Really. Don't worry, Dad.'

'I'm not worrying,' Christian said mildly, 'but I think you should go to the disco. All your friends will be going, presumably?'

'I don't know. I suppose so.'

'Then you should go, too.'

Chloe threw an anguished look towards Lara. 'It finishes so late.'

'One of us will pick you up,' she said immediately.

'I'd rather stay at home.'

At that moment Aggie came running towards them, still dressed in her angel costume and white ballet shoes. She was clutching two big bags. 'I can go home like this if I like. Daddy, will you take me for an ice cream? Can I stay in my costume?'

'Great idea,' Christian drawled, scooping her into his arms. 'After all, it's only minus two degrees outside. Eating an ice cream half-naked seems perfectly logical. Why don't you and Lara go shopping, Chloe? We'll see you later.'

Chloe stared at him for a moment and then blinked several times. 'OK,' she said huskily. 'We'll go shopping.'

'This will look great on you. Try it.' It was Lara's fourth attempt to persuade Chloe to try on a dress.

Listlessly, Chloe stared at the dress and shook her head. 'I don't need anything new.'

Lara put the dress down and sat down on the seat in the cubicle. 'All right. Enough. What's wrong with the clothes? Am I picking the wrong things for you?'

'No, everything is great,' Chloe said quickly. 'I just— don't need anything.'

'Would you rather have gone for an ice cream with your dad?' Lara narrowed her eyes. 'I'm missing something here. Chloe, what's wrong?'

Suddenly a hideous thought occurred to her.

Had Chloe guessed how Lara felt about her father?

Was she feeling insecure?

To her horror, the girl's eyes filled with tears. 'Nothing. I just don't want to spend Daddy's money. I have everything I need.' And with that she fumbled her way out of the changing room, leaving Lara staring after her in bemusement and concern.

She abandoned the dress she was holding and sprinted after her. 'Chloe, wait. Wait!' She caught her just outside the shop and grabbed her arm. 'Please, don't run away from me. We have to talk. If there's something worrying you then talk to me. Please.'

'There's nothing to say.'

'Well, if you won't talk to me, at least talk to your dad,' Lara urged, wishing they weren't in the middle of a busy shopping centre, heaving with Christmas shoppers. 'He's worried about you.'

Chloe's eyes widened and she shook her head. 'I don't want him to be worried about me.'

'Of course you do. *He's your dad!* A daughter's role in life is to worry her dad!'

'He isn't my dad.'

Christmas carols wailed out of the loudspeakers in the shopping centre and a bag dug into the back of Lara's leg as shoppers elbowed past them, but she didn't even notice. 'What do you mean, he isn't your dad? Of course he's your dad.'

'No.' Chloe shook her head violently. 'Christian married my mum. And they had Aggie. Aggie is his child. I'm not.'

Lara opened her mouth and closed it again, wondering why Christian had never thought to mention that fact. 'I don't know what to say.' Her voice came out in a croak. 'He's never mentioned it.'

'He never does. He's far too kind.' Chloe looked away from her, staring blankly into the middle distance as the crowds of shoppers poured around them. 'It was really decent of him to let me live with him after Mum left.'

'Hold on a minute.' Lara lifted a hand to slow the conversation and then turned to glare at a woman who bashed into them. 'Excuse me!'

'It's not a good place to stand, love,' the woman returned, and Lara grabbed Chloe's arm.

'She's right. We can't have a proper conversation with the entire world tramping over us as they do their Christmas shopping. And, if they play that Rudolph song again, I'm going to hang myself from the nearest piece of tinsel. Come on. You and I are going to have a proper talk.' She dragged Chloe back to the car park and drove her home. 'Your dad and Aggie are eating ice cream so we can have five minutes by ourselves. I'll make my special hot chocolate and we'll take it up to your bedroom.'

Once home, she made them both a drink and Chloe helped her carry the mugs up to her bedroom.

Lara slipped off her shoes and curled up on the bed. 'Right. Tell me everything. And don't hold anything back. It seems to me that you've got far too much bottled up inside you.'

Chloe sat down next to her, her hands round her mug of chocolate. 'I don't usually talk about it to anyone.'

'I'm not just anyone and you're going to talk about it with me. Go.'

Chloe hesitated. 'I was four and a half when Dad met my mum.'

'What happened to your real father?'

'He didn't want children.' Chloe poked the spoon into her hot chocolate. 'So I guess I spoiled that relationship for her.'

Lara's eyes narrowed. 'How do you know he didn't want children?'

'Well, he isn't exactly around, is he?' Chloe sighed. 'Sorry. I didn't mean to be snappy.'

'Don't apologise. You finally sounded like a moody teenager. It's a relief to hear it.'

'You want me to be moody?'

'No,' Lara said softly. 'I want you to be yourself.'

Chloe stared at her and her eyes filled. 'I can't.'

'Oh, sweetheart…' Lara leaned forward and removed the mug of chocolate from Chloe's fingers. She put it on the bedside table and stretched out her arms. 'Give me a hug.'

Chloe hesitated and then slid into her arms and Lara felt the child's skinny body tremble with repressed emotion. 'I'm *so* scared, Lara.' She burst into tears and Lara tightened her grip.

She let her cry for a few minutes and then tried to unwrap herself from Chloe's grasp so that she could get a better look at her. 'Chloe—look at me. You have to talk to me so that I can help. I just don't know what's going on here. What are you scared of?'

Chloe was sobbing so hard that her response was unintelligible but Lara thought it sounded like, 'Isn't it obvious?'

'Obvious? No. Not to me.' Seriously concerned, Lara kept one arm round the child and reached across to the bedside table so that she could grab a tissue from the box. 'Here. Blow.'

Chloe peeled herself away from Lara's neck and took the tissue. 'I'm afraid he doesn't…really…want…me.' Her voice juddered and she stopped talking and blew her nose hard.

'Who doesn't want you? You have to stop crying, Chloe. You'll give yourself a horrible headache.'

'My dad.' Chloe's voice was clogged with tears. 'Because he isn't really my dad, is he? I mean…' Just saying the words was enough to set her off sobbing again. 'My mum just walked out. Just like that. And left me here. And that's fine because, to be honest, if she'd given me a choice I would have chosen to live with my dad any day because he always has time for me and she never did.' She scrubbed the heel of her hand across her cheek and drew in a shuddering breath. 'But he probably wouldn't have chosen to keep me.'

'Chloe!' Genuinely shocked, Lara gave her a gentle shake. 'Your dad *adores* you.' She'd seen the evidence repeatedly.

'No. He didn't have any choice, Lara,' Chloe sobbed. 'She just walked out and *dumped* me on him. He always has to think about us. His whole life revolves around us. And I'm sure he hates being a parent as much as she did.'

'No.' Lara shook her head, appalled. 'I'm equally sure that he doesn't. *He loves you.*'

'I make his life more difficult. I try not to, but—'

'Is that why you're always trying to please me?' Christian's voice came from the doorway, hoarse and disbelieving.

Chloe jumped to her feet in horror. 'Dad! We didn't know you were home.' She made a frantic attempt to brush the tears from her face. 'We were just— We were—'

'Finally telling the truth?' Christian's face was white. 'Chloe, how could you possibly think those things? What have I ever done to give you the impression that I don't love you?'

His gaze slid briefly to Lara and she knew that he was thinking the same thing that she'd been thinking—*that the intensity of their relationship had somehow communicated itself to the children.*

Chloe collapsed onto Lara and started to sob again. 'Mum didn't want me and she's actually *related* to me. It was *all* my fault you split up, because she got fed up with having a family. She told me that, if she had her time again, she wouldn't have children. So why would you want to be stuck with me? *I'm not even yours!*' She cried and cried and then Lara felt the bed beside them dip as Christian sat down.

'Angel, we have to have a serious talk.' He rubbed a

hand gently down Chloe's back. 'Let go of Lara and stop crying. Look at me.'

'I'm sorry. I'm sorry.' Chloe clutched at Lara, crying so hard that she was almost incoherent. 'I don't mean to make a fuss.'

'Chloe.' Christian's voice was firm and this time he put his arms round the child and lifted her onto his own lap. 'Sweetheart, you have to try and calm down so that we can talk properly. You're making Lara cry, too.'

'Sorry,' Lara muttered, wiping her cheek with the palm of her hand and giving him an apologetic look. 'It's just all a bit…emotional.'

'Can everyone stop saying *sorry?*' Christian gently but firmly held Chloe while she cried. 'Please, try and stop crying, angel. I want you to listen to me. Let's start this from the beginning. The most important thing to say is that you *are* mine. And I don't ever want you ever to believe anything different.'

'But—'

'You're *mine*.' Christian's voice was firm. 'Mine. Now, onto the second point. Your mother left, yes. But you weren't to blame.'

'Oh, come on, Dad.' Chloe eased away from him and gave a tiny laugh. 'Mum hated being a mum.'

Christian shook her head. 'She didn't hate being a mum. It's true that she didn't like staying at home, but it was nothing to do with you, baby. Your mum was addicted to her work.' He hesitated. 'It's really hard to explain, but work made her feel good. It made her feel good in a way that nothing else did, including me. If anyone is to blame for the fact that she left, then it's me. She needed something that I just couldn't seem to give her.'

'But the job was more appealing than Aggie and me,'

Chloe said in a soft voice. '"Having kids is relentless." She told me that once. She said that having kids was all about putting yourself second. Now *you're* the one putting yourself second.'

'I don't put myself second.'

'You're always thinking of us.'

'Because I love you,' Christian said, stroking her hair away from her face with a gentle hand. 'Not because it's a sacrifice.'

'It *must* be a sacrifice. You're not even my real dad. You're only stuck with me because you married my mum.'

Christian's jaw tensed. 'I'm going to tell you something I should have told you years ago. I fell in love with you on the first day I met you, Chloe. You were so sweet, loving and thoughtful and such fun to be with. I never wanted to let you go. Don't ever say I'm not your real dad because you'll break my heart.' His voice was hoarse. 'You're my daughter every bit as much as Aggie is, and no dad could ever love you more than I do.'

'You don't have to keep me,' Chloe whispered in a small voice, and Christian was silent for a moment. Then he cleared his throat.

'Sweetheart, I wouldn't part with you if someone offered me the sun and the moon. You're my family. Don't you dare ever think differently.'

Chloe stared at him for a moment, her whole body trembling. And then she leaned forward and flung her arms round his neck. 'Oh, Daddy, Daddy,' she sobbed into his neck, 'I love you so much and I've been so frightened since Mum left.'

Christian smoothed his hand over her head, his jaw clenched tight as he struggled for control. 'I should have realised. I knew something was wrong but I just thought you were upset about your mum leaving,' he said huskily. 'You should have told me how you felt. I can't believe you didn't tell me. Because I think of you as my daughter, it didn't occur to me that you'd be worrying.'

Chloe sobbed and sobbed. 'I thought if I was bad I might have to leave you and Aggie and I love you both. I love you, Daddy.'

'And I love you, too. And I would never, ever do anything that would hurt you.'

Lara rubbed the tears from her cheeks and stood up, feeling numb inside.

She knew that whatever she felt for Christian had to end, here and now. She'd glimpsed the depths of Chloe's trauma and finally she understood his refusal to introduce more change into his daughters' lives.

He was right.

It would be too much for them.

How could she expect the children to take on yet another change when their lives had already been so cruelly disrupted? How could she expect Chloe to share her father with another woman? The child needed the security of knowing that she had no competition for his affection.

And Lara had no intention of hurting his children.

'I need to sort out some things in my room,' she muttered, moving towards the door, intent on leaving them together.

'Lara.' Christian's voice was soft. 'Thank you.'

Chloe turned her head, her face blotched and her eyes swollen from crying. 'Yes, thank you. If it hadn't been for you, I never would have said anything.'

Lara managed a smile. 'You would have got there in the end,' she said quietly. 'You're a very close family. And close families always find a way.'

CHAPTER ELEVEN

'HAVE you heard the latest?' Jane waltzed into the staff-room. 'Jack's wife gave birth to a baby boy this morning. Mother and baby doing well.'

'A baby *boy*?' Rousing herself out of a state of misery, Lara managed a smile, knowing that she was referring to the psychic's prediction. 'She was having a girl.'

'They got it wrong.' Jane grinned. 'Now I expect you're spooked.'

'Oh, of course.' Lara rolled her eyes and turned her attention back to her coffee. 'I'll be delivering my own quads any moment now. Don't be ridiculous, Jane, the psychic didn't say anything about me meeting a man with trau-matised children.'

'I know, I know. It's all nonsense. Oh, well, only two days until Christmas,' Jane murmured as she rummaged in the fridge for some milk that hadn't passed its sell-by date.

'That's right.' Lara finished her coffee and stood up. 'And only three weeks until I go to Australia.'

Jane turned and looked at her. 'You're going, then?'

'Of course.' Lara turned her back and quickly washed her mug. 'Why wouldn't I?'

'I thought—I hoped… You don't have to be a genius to

sense that something's happened between you and Christian.'

'Oh. Is it that obvious?'

'You haven't managed to cure yourself, then?'

Lara stood for a moment, feeling numb. 'No.' She turned to Jane and flashed her a smile. 'But don't tell my mother.'

'But if you love him—'

'I don't just love him.' Lara abandoned her mug in the sink and wrapped her arms around herself to try and inject some warmth into her shivering body. She felt cold. *So cold.* 'I also love his girls. And they're the reason that nothing is going to happen between us. It can't.'

'But what if they—?'

'They've had a very traumatic experience.' *Only will-power stopped her from sobbing as Chloe had.* 'I only recently realised just how traumatic. There's no way I'm going to be responsible for rocking their little world a second time when they've only just found their feet. They deserve stability.'

There was a long silence and then she felt Jane's hand on her shoulder. 'In that case, I'm sorry. I'm *really* sorry it didn't work out.'

Lara squeezed her eyes shut and tried to hold back the tears. 'One of those things. Life showing its sense of humour. Right man. Wrong circumstances.'

'Just focus on his flaws. Did you ever find one, by the way?'

'Oh, yes.' Lara hesitated and then gave a sad smile. 'His flaw was that he was unavailable.'

Jane sighed. 'You don't think if you—'

'No.' Lara interrupted her quickly. 'I don't. Anyway, back to work. Where do you want me? Resus? I don't quite know what I'm going to do when I leave here. Will I know how to occupy my time when I'm not surrounded by bleeping machines and injured patients?'

'You'll have a great time with your brother and then you'll meet a fit, healthy Australian male who will take your mind off everything.' Jane's voice was falsely bright and Lara looked at her.

'Yes. That's what I'm going to do. You're a good friend. Have I told you that lately?'

Jane leaned forward and gave her a hug. 'You're going to be all right.'

Was she?

Maybe. One day.

And in the meantime she was going to put one foot in front of the other, do her job and try and forget just how much love hurt.

Why had he agreed to ice-skating?

Christian watched as Lara made slow circles on the ice, as poised and graceful as a ballerina, her hands carefully guiding an excited Aggie.

'Look at me, Daddy!' Aggie's voice echoed across the ice as she wobbled precariously, her bottom sticking out. 'If Lara skates backwards, I can do it!'

'You should try it, Dad!' Chloe sailed past him, arms whirling, and crashed into the side of the ice rink. She turned to him with a grin, laughter brightening her face. 'This is *brilliant*. Lara hasn't taught me how to turn yet.'

Christian pushed his hands deeper in his coat pockets. It was wonderful to see Chloe so relaxed and unselfconscious.

Since her emotional confession, they'd turned a corner. She'd blossomed.

Thanks to Lara.

Lara was skating on her own now, executing spins and turns that made Aggie gasp and clap her hands with delight.

'Look at Lara, Daddy!'

He was looking.

'You like her, don't you, Dad?' Chloe's voice came from right next to him and he tried to keep his smile casual, cursing himself for being so obvious.

'Of course. Who couldn't not like Lara? She's a nice girl.'

'Girl?' Chloe gave him a disbelieving look. 'She isn't a girl, Dad! She's a woman.'

Memories of the hot, passionate interlude in his office filled his brain and he loosened his scarf. *He knew she was a woman.*

Aggie slid up to them, her arms outstretched like a tight-rope walker as she struggled to keep her balance.

Christian caught her and lifted her over the barrier and into his arms, skates and all. 'So—have you had enough?'

'I'm *starving.*' Aggie was breathless and her cheeks were pink. 'Lara said they sell hot chocolate here. It won't be as good as hers, but can we have some? *Please?*'

Lara skated towards them and glided to an elegant stop in front of the barrier. 'Hot chocolate?'

Was it his imagination or had he seen less of her since that night?

She'd been busy, of course, but still…

'Can I sit by you, Lara?' Aggie reached out her arms and Christian frowned and held on to her.

'Lara can't carry you. You're too heavy.'

'I'll walk, then. I want to hold her hand.' Aggie wriggled and Christian removed her skates and put her down.

They found a table for four right next to the ice rink and Christian ordered while Lara and the girls watched the skaters.

'She's good,' Lara said, as a girl with a ponytail spun past them.

'Not as good as you.' Aggie crawled onto her lap. 'Where did you learn to skate?'

'At school.'

'Wow. I wish they did cool things like that at our school. We only do boring netball.'

A waitress walked up to their table with a loaded tray. 'Muffins, chocolate brownies, three hot chocolates and a mulled wine?'

'I'm drinking the alcohol,' Christian drawled, and the waitress smiled and put the drinks on the table.

'You look as though you're all having fun.'

'It's amazing,' Aggie breathed, and the waitress studied her and then Chloe.

'It's nice to see a family out together. You girls look exactly like your mother.' She smiled at Lara. 'Taking a break from the Christmas shopping and the turkey?'

Christian froze and Aggie frowned.

'She isn't our mother.'

'Oh.' The waitress looked embarrassed. 'I'm sorry. I just assumed—You look so alike— Call me if there's anything else you need.' Her face scarlet, she hurried back towards the bar area, obviously eager to escape from her gaffe.

Aggie was silent for a moment and then stared at her sister. 'Why would she think that Lara is our mummy?'

Chloe didn't answer. Instead, she sat in silence, a slight frown on her face.

Then she glanced at Christian, a question in her eyes.

He managed what he hoped was a reassuring smile. 'Everything's fine, sweetheart. You have nothing to worry about.'

But Chloe carried on staring and for an uncomfortable

moment he had the feeling that she could see right into his soul.

She was obviously worried that her life was going to be disrupted again and Lara clearly picked up the same signals because she put down her mug of chocolate and laughed.

'It's because we're all blonde and wrapped up in scarves! She can't see us properly. Anyone with two eyes in their head can see we don't look the same. I have freckles, for a start, and my nose turns up at the end. You two are much more beautiful. Anyway, forget that. Come on, guys.' Lara lifted Aggie onto the floor and jumped to her feet, her eyes sparkling. 'I'm going to teach you both to skate backwards. It's dead easy once you get the hang of it and it looks *so* cool.'

With no apparent effort she'd defused the tension around the table and bent down to help the girls put on their skates.

Christian studied her face, searching for clues as to whether she was upset, but it was impossible to tell because she was concentrating on his children and didn't once glance in his direction.

In no time at all they were back on the ice and she took it in turns to teach the children to skate backwards.

The children giggled and shrieked and were obviously having an amazing time and Christian watched, wondering whether their happiness was going to be at the expense of his own.

It snowed again overnight and Christmas Eve was busy in the emergency department.

'People should be at home, decorating their trees,' Jane muttered as she directed yet another patient towards X-Ray.

Lara nodded. 'Can I ask you a favour?'

'Ask.'

'Can I run the treatment room today? I need a break from Resus.'

There was a long silence. 'You're finding it that hard to work with him?'

'Actually, yes.' Lara didn't bother with excuses or denials. 'Pathetic, no?'

'Not pathetic.' Jane let out a long breath. 'I'll put Helen in Resus. But you know he'll probably ask for you. He always does.'

'There are plenty of good nurses in this department. And I'm only here for another few weeks.'

'Yes.'

At that moment Fran came dashing up to them, her hand over her mouth. 'Oh, my—you'll never guess what!'

Jane and Lara glanced at each other and then back at the receptionist. 'What?'

'I'm pregnant!'

Lara swallowed and Jane started to laugh. 'You are joking.'

'No.' Fran shook her head, tears in her eyes. 'I'm pregnant. *I'm pregnant.* That psychic woman said I'd be pregnant by Christmas and *she was right*. Can you believe it? At the time I thought she was delusional, but she obviously knew what she was talking about.'

Without giving either of them the time to respond, Fran danced off down the corridor in search of someone else to tell.

Jane cleared her throat. 'She's obviously pleased, then, is she?'

Lara was staring at Fran's retreating form with an expression of disbelief on her face. 'Tell me she doesn't think she's pregnant because of the psychic. I mean—she does know the facts about human reproduction, I assume?'

'Well, you've got to agree that it's a spooky coincidence. I mean, first Jack has a little boy, even though the scan said it was a girl. And then Fran gets pregnant.' Jane was smiling. 'All that's left is that for you to—' She broke off and Lara gave her a withering look.

'Oh, please! Give me a break! On second thoughts, *you* take a break. If you're starting to believe what a psychic tells you then you obviously need one. I'm going to bury myself in the treatment room and I'm staying there until it's time to go home.'

But talking to Jane about leaving got her thinking and during her lunch-break she followed up some calls she'd made earlier in the week to nanny agencies. If she was going to Australia, she needed to find Christian some help.

By the end of her shift she was tired and, when she saw Christian standing in the doorway, her heart sank.

Not now.

'Everything all right?' She threw the remains of the dressing pack into the bin and washed her hands.

'Have you been avoiding me?'

'Of course not,' she lied, 'far from it. In fact, I wanted to talk to you.'

He walked into the room and let the door swing shut behind him. 'I'm listening.'

She forced herself to continue tidying. It was the only way to be absolutely sure that she wouldn't embarrass herself by throwing herself at him. 'I've been asking round the hospital. One of the staff nurses on Paeds had an excellent nanny-housekeeper who's leaving in January. She'd be perfect for you. I could help you interview her, if you like, before I go.'

He frowned. 'Lara—'

'Obviously I have *loads* of things to do before I go to

Australia. If we could persuade her to start immediately in January, I'd have time to clear out my flat and pack. If she could move in more or less straight away, that would be perfect.'

'*Lara!*'

'Don't!' She lifted a hand to stop him speaking, but didn't turn to look at him. *She didn't dare.* 'Don't say a word, Christian. It was special, we both know that. But it was also impossible. I finally understood that the other night, when I had Chloe sobbing in my arms. You've done such a good job as a father and because of you, the girls have weathered the trauma of your marriage break-up remarkably well. But I can see now that you're right. They don't need to worry that they're fighting with someone for your affections.'

She stood for a moment, desperately hoping that he wouldn't argue with her.

Desperately hoping that he would.

But he said nothing at all and, when she heard the door crash, she glanced round and discovered that he'd gone.

'I've labelled my stocking because I absolutely don't want to get Chloe's toys.' Aggie carefully placed her stocking by the fireplace. 'Do you think this is the right place?'

'It looks good to me.' Christian glanced around him. The lights on the tree twinkled and the scent of cinnamon and cloves filled the sitting room. Twists of holly adorned the fireplace and candles flickered, creating a warm, cosy atmosphere. The huge comfy sofas were covered in toys and books that the children had been reading.

The boxes were gone and the whole house felt lived in. *Thanks to Lara.*

Aggie was looking at him. 'Can we leave a carrot for Rudolph?'

'Carrot? I didn't think to buy any.' Christian wondered what else he'd missed. How was he supposed to know all these things?

'Lara bought some. I saw a bag in the fridge.' Aggie dashed off to the kitchen and returned with a carrot which she placed carefully in front of the fire. 'For Rudolph. And one of Lara's amazing mince pies for Father Christmas.'

'Where is Lara?' Chloe was sewing her name on her stocking. 'I haven't seen her since supper.'

'I expect she had things to do in her room.'

'Have you bought Lara a present?' Aggie stared at him, wide-eyed. 'Did you forget?'

Christian felt a flicker of guilt. 'Actually, I *did* forget.'

Lara had helped with all his Christmas shopping and he doubted that she'd remembered to include anything for herself.

'You forgot?' Aggie looked appalled. 'How could you forget?'

Because the last thing on his mind had been Christmas presents. All he could think about was being with Lara. And *not* being with her. It didn't matter what he happened to be doing at the time, he couldn't get her out of his mind.

'It isn't too late. The shops don't shut for another two hours.' Aggie scrambled to her feet, bouncy and excited. 'We can dash out now and buy something special.'

But he probably should have bought her something. She'd transformed his home, hadn't she? She'd helped Chloe. It was because of her that he, Chloe and Aggie felt like a family.

'She's going abroad, Aggie. She doesn't need anything.'

Silence followed his words.

'Can't she stay?' Aggie drooped. 'It would be really great if she could stay as our nanny. She never yells at us to tidy up and last week I found my homework under a pile of *her* clothes. She's *so* cool.'

'She can't be your nanny, Aggie.' Christian kept his tone matter-of-fact. 'But she and I have found a new nanny who is going to start in January. I think you'll like her.'

'I don't want a new nanny. I love Lara.' Aggie's lip wobbled and her voice was plaintive. 'Don't you love Lara, Daddy?'

He froze and for a moment found himself totally unable to deliver the answer he knew that he had to deliver. And then his attention was caught by the stricken, panicked look on Chloe's face.

Her sudden insecurity was obvious in her eyes.

'Love?' Driven by concern for his daughter, he found the words he'd been searching for. 'Of course not. Lara is great. She's a fun, lovely person.'

Chloe was still staring at him. 'Dad?' Her voice was hoarse. 'You know you said that we should always be honest and say if something is worrying us?'

Christian tensed. It was obvious what was worrying her.

'You don't have anything to worry about, sweetheart. Your new nanny will be fine. Lara will soon be gone.' Just saying the words made his insides feel hollow, and Chloe shook her head.

'You don't know what I want to say.'

Oh, yes, he did.

She intended to spell it out. She was going to beg him not to marry again and he was going to assure him that he wouldn't.

'All right, Chloe.' His voice was gentle as he ruthlessly

buried his own emotions. 'Say what's worrying you, angel, and we'll deal with it, I promise.'

'Wake up, wake up, *he's been*!'

Lara opened her eyes to find Aggie bouncing on the bed, her blonde curls swinging around her smiling face.

'Who's been?'

'Now you're being silly.' Aggie gurgled with laughter and tugged at the duvet. 'You *know* who's been. Come on. Get up. You need to come and see.'

Lara dutifully sat up and rubbed her eyes. Had she slept at all? It felt as though she'd spent the whole night staring at the ceiling, thinking about Christian, but at some point she must have fallen asleep.

Her head throbbed and her heart ached.

Spending Christmas with them was going to make it so much harder to leave when the time came.

'Don't be sad,' Aggie said, dragging her by the hand. 'I wrote to Father Christmas and told him that you were a good person and he's left you loads of presents. And there's something really special, but I'm not allowed to tell you what it is because Chloe says she'll strangle me if I do.'

'Oh? He's left me presents?' Lara yawned, careful not to reveal that she knew exactly what was waiting for them under the tree. She and Christian had spent an hour wrapping presents two nights previously.

Neither of them had spoken a word.

At one point their fingers had brushed and the chemistry had ignited between them but Lara had quickly retreated to her present-wrapping, knowing that they didn't dare risk touching each other while the girls were in the house.

And, anyway, she didn't think she was emotionally robust enough to make love with him again and then walk away.

Aggie peeped up at her. 'It's supposed to be a surprise but I could whisper about your present if you like and you can pretend you don't know.'

Driven by an impulse that she couldn't control, Lara knelt down and hugged her. 'If it's supposed to be a surprise then you'd better not tell me,' she said huskily. 'Hold onto your secret a bit longer.'

'You're squeezing me *really* tight!' Aggie wriggled in her grasp and Lara blinked rapidly and released her.

'Sorry!'

Aggie dragged her into the sitting room and Christian was already there, sprawled on the sofa in an ancient pair of jeans and a soft cotton T-shirt that draped itself lovingly over his broad shoulders. The dark stubble on his jaw suggested that he'd also been dragged unceremoniously out of bed. Chloe was next to him, laughing and giggling.

Like a different child, Lara thought as she smiled at them both and knelt down on the floor.

Christian seemed happy and relaxed. More relaxed than she could ever recall seeing him.

And she was pleased for him.

Today he was a father, enjoying Christmas with his girls.

He glanced up at her and for a long moment they just stared at each other, and then something flickered in his blue eyes. 'Good morning, Lara. Merry Christmas.'

'Merry Christmas.' Suddenly she wished Aggie had given her time to have a shower and wash her hair.

A lazy smile touched his mouth as he reached across and handed her a large mug of coffee. 'Take it. It's strong. If you feel anything like I do, you need it.'

'I expect you're both tired because you were so excited about Father Christmas coming. Were you awake all night?

I was.' Aggie was under the tree, yanking out presents. 'What do we open first? Can I open this huge one?'

'Only if it has your name on it,' Christian said mildly, shaking his head as he watched his daughter. 'I think she's going to explode in a minute.'

'Aggie, let's start with the stockings,' Chloe said, sticking her hand in and pulling out a strangely shaped parcel.

The next hour passed in a haze of laughter, wrapping paper and excited children.

When the entire sitting room was covered in paper and discarded packaging, they went outside and 'discovered' Aggie's new bike.

'Father Christmas was listening,' she said happily, as she careered down the snowy path on her bright red bike. 'This is brilliant. Listen to the bell.'

Leaving them to enjoy themselves, Lara sneaked out to put the turkey in the oven.

From the garden she could hear the sounds of Aggie and Chloe laughing, interspersed with Christian's deeper tones.

She looked round his beautiful kitchen and felt a lump settle in her throat.

She'd never thought this would happen to her.

She'd honestly never thought she'd meet a man who would make her want to just abandon everything and settle down.

Blinking back tears, she slid the turkey into the oven and closed the door. Would she ever find another man who would make her feel this way?

'Lara.' Aggie's voice came from the sitting room. 'You have to come! We're waiting for you! It's your turn!'

Her turn for what?

Lara closed her eyes briefly. Somehow she had to get through the day.

The children were happy and excited and they didn't need her miserable face spoiling their fun.

Taking a deep breath, she pinned a smile on her face and walked back into the room.

'Here I am. What's the problem?'

'You haven't opened your stocking.' Aggie was hopping around and Chloe frowned at her and grabbed her hand.

'Be quiet, Aggie! For once in your life, *stop talking!* Daddy has to do this bit.'

Aggie gave a hopeless whimper. 'But we *all* helped choose the presents and I—'

'Aggie!' Chloe's tone was sharp. 'Enough!'

Aggie subsided and Lara glanced between the three of them, baffled. 'What's going on?'

Chloe cleared her throat. 'Daddy has something that he wants to give you.'

Lara pulled a face. 'Well—this is embarrassing,' she muttered, casting an apologetic glance in his direction. 'Sorry. I sort of assumed that you knew not to buy me anything.'

'It's a stocking,' Aggie breathed, her eyes shining with excitement. 'More than one thing.'

Lara's eyes slid to the fireplace and, sure enough, there was a small stocking with her name on it. She swallowed down the lump in her throat. 'That's so sweet of you all,' she croaked, walking across to pick it up. 'Gosh. I don't know what to say.'

Aggie darted towards her. 'Do you want me to help you open the presents?'

'Aggie!' Christian and Chloe spoke simultaneously, and Lara laughed.

She sat down on the sofa and pulled the little girl onto her lap. 'Actually, I'd love some help,' she said, reaching into the stocking and pulling out the first present. Smiling at Aggie, she rattled it and sniffed it and then squeezed it. 'Interesting shape.'

'Open it.'

Lara dutifully opened it and found a set of keys. Intrigued and puzzled, she glanced at Christian. 'Keys? Keys to what?'

'Open the next present,' he ordered softly, and she blushed, wishing he wouldn't look at her with such blatant masculine appreciation.

The children were going to notice.

Wondering why on earth they'd given her a set of keys, she reached for the next present and opened it. It was a travel brochure.

Even more baffled, she glanced at them. 'I don't understand…'

Chloe was smiling. 'You have to open all of the presents before we tell you.'

Tell her what?

'Open the next present.' Christian was smiling, too, and Lara pushed her hand into the stocking and retrieved the final item. It was a small box, beautifully wrapped in glittery paper and tied with ribbon.

'It's pretty,' Lara murmured, glancing towards the keys and the travel brochure, wondering what to make of them. She hadn't had enough sleep for riddles.

'Open it, open it.' Aggie bounced on her lap and grabbed at the small box. 'I'll help you.'

'No!' Chloe dashed forward and gave the box back to Lara. 'She has to open it herself.'

'But she's *so* slow.' Aggie whimpered with impatience. 'Can you open it quickly?'

Lara obligingly slid her finger under the tape, freed the box from its packaging and flipped it open.

And gasped with shock, because there, nestling in a
bed of blue velvet, was a ring.

But not just any ring.

It was the biggest, most beautiful diamond solitaire
she'd ever seen, and it flashed and winked at her as if determined to catch her attention.

Dumb with astonishment, Lara lifted her head and met
Christian's eyes.

They stayed like that for a moment, just gazing at each
other, and then Aggie flung her arms around her neck.

'Daddy wants you to marry him. Are you going to say
yes? We're not sure if you're going to say yes. Please, say
yes. If I promise not to talk too much, will you say yes?'

'Aggie!' Appalled, Chloe glared at her sister. 'You've
just ruined everything! Daddy is supposed to do the asking, not you!'

'But he was taking so long!' Aggie's lip started to wobble and Lara cuddled her closer, her eyes still on Christian,
who was smiling.

He looked happy and relaxed, as if an enormous load
had been lifted from his shoulders.

'Well?' His voice was soft as his gaze held hers.
'Aggie asked you a question. Are you going to give her
an answer?'

Lara tried to breathe. 'You— I…' She stared down at
the ring. 'This is for me?'

'If you don't like it, we can change it.'

Chloe pulled a face at her father. 'That's not very romantic! You're supposed to go on one knee, Dad. Put the
ring on her finger.' She shook her head in disbelief. 'You're
a grown-up! You're supposed to know all this stuff!'

'Am I?' Christian was still watching Lara. 'Do you want
me on my knees? Because if that's what it takes, I'll do it.'

Chloe groaned. 'Don't ask, Daddy. Just do it!'

Lara glanced at Chloe and saw the yearning in the girl's face.

'We can't— It's too much for— You've had so much disruption and insecurity— You don't need more change.' She was nearly incoherent and Aggie peered at her.

'You sound a bit like Nanny Bottle when she was thirsty. Her words came out in the wrong order, too.'

Lara gave a strangled laugh and hugged Aggie. 'I'm not thirsty, I'm just…shocked. I wasn't expecting…this. I just don't think you need any more change in your lives.'

'If you leave, things will change,' Chloe said quietly, sliding onto the sofa next to her. 'And that's not a change that any of us want. Will you stay? Marry Daddy? I know he still hasn't got round to telling you, but he loves you. That's what the presents are. The key is to our front door, it's yours for ever.'

'And the magazine is so that you can pick a holiday to go on when we're all married,' Aggie intervened, and Chloe sighed.

'It's called a honeymoon. And she isn't marrying all of us. She's marrying Daddy.'

'She *is* marrying all of us!'

Lara looked at Christian, unable to believe what was happening. 'A honeymoon?'

'I know you need to go to Australia to see your brother, but will you come straight back, instead of travelling? And then we'll have a honeymoon.'

There was a long silence and Lara swallowed. 'I—I didn't think this could possibly happen. I thought it would be too much for the children.' It was so enormous—so perfect—that she didn't dare believe it. 'We agreed that it would be best if I just left.'

'I was wrong about that. The girls love you, too, Lara. As much as I do.'

His words made her heart skip several beats. 'You love me, Christian?'

'Of course he does.' Aggie beamed at her. 'And we love you, too. You make great mince pies and you taught us to skate backwards. And you make more mess in the house than we do. Your only bad thing is that you cook me broccoli.'

Half laughing, half crying, Lara looked at Christian. *'You love me?'*

'Do you doubt it? All right, enough of marriage proposals by consensus. Move over, Aggie, it's my turn.' Lifting his youngest daughter off Lara's lap, he put her gently on the floor. Then he pulled Lara to her feet. 'Girls, go and make your beds.'

Aggie frowned. 'I already made my bed.'

Christian's eyes were on Lara's face. 'Then go and unmake it.'

'But I want to watch—'

'Aggie, come on!' Chloe dragged her protesting sister from the room and Lara dragged her gaze away from Christian's and glanced after them.

'I don't want to throw them out of the sitting room on Christmas Day.'

'It's only for a minute.' He cupped her face in his hands and lowered his mouth to hers. 'This has to have been the most unconventional proposal of marriage ever. But I suppose it's a reflection of what I'm offering you. You'd be marrying more than just me, Lara. It's a lot to take on. If you're going to say yes then you have to know what you're saying yes to.'

'I love you, Christian, and I love your girls.' She flung her arms around his neck and tears spilled down her cheeks. *'Our* girls. I know what I'm saying yes to.'

His grip tightened. 'You're saying yes?'

Her voice was clogged with tears of happiness. 'Did you really think I wouldn't?'

'You were excited about your trip to Australia.'

'That was until I fell in love with you. Then I couldn't bear the thought of leaving you. I've been so miserable.'

'Stop crying.' His expression amused and concerned at the same time, he brushed the tears away from her face. 'This is supposed to be a happy moment.'

'It *is* a happy moment. But it's also an unexpected moment. I couldn't see any sort of future for us.' She sniffed. 'I thought you didn't want to unsettle the children.'

'It turned out that they were more unsettled by the thought of you going than staying.' He slid his fingers through her hair. 'Clearly we weren't as good at hiding our feelings as we thought we were. Chloe sat me down and forced me to admit how I felt about you.'

'She did? When?'

'Yesterday, when you were upstairs. They informed me that they wanted me to marry you.'

'Ah…' She smiled up at him. 'So none of this was your idea?'

'I admit I had some help.' He gave a slow, sexy smile and slid the ring onto her finger. 'So you like it? The girls thought it was "cool".'

Lara swallowed as she looked at the size of it. 'I hope you haven't sold the house to pay for it.'

'He didn't have to. Daddy has lots of money.' Aggie danced into the room with Chloe close behind. 'He's very rich.'

'Is he?' Lara started to laugh. 'My mother is never going to believe this!'

'Will you have a baby now?' Aggie's voice was

innocent. 'Chloe and I would love a baby sister. Or a brother. We're not fussy.'

Christian closed his eyes briefly and then sent her a look of apology. 'Sorry,' he murmured. 'Do you think you're up to this or is it going to be too much for you?'

Lara couldn't stop smiling. 'Oh, I'm definitely up to it. And on the subject of children, there's something that I think I'd better tell you while there's still time for you to change your mind.'

His expression curious, he stroked a hand over her cheek. 'Go on. But I ought to warn you that nothing is going to make me change my mind.'

'Did I ever mention a patient who was a psychic?'

'No.' He lowered his head and kissed her gently. 'Do we have to talk about work?'

'Well, this isn't exactly work. She came into the department a month ago and she predicted that Fran would be pregnant by Christmas and that Jack would have a boy, not a girl, and that I—' She broke off and Christian looked at her expectantly.

'And you?' He lifted an eyebrow in question. 'What did she predict for you?'

'I was just coming to that part.' Lara's eyes twinkled with wicked humour. 'I think you might want to sit down, Dr Blake…'